Cauldrons and Corpses

Nola Robertson

Copyright © 2020 Nola Robertson

ISBN-13: 978-1-953213-11-2

Also by Nola Robertson

The Tarron Hunter Series

Hunter Claimed
Hunter Enslaved
Hunter Unchained
Hunter Forbidden
Hunter Scorned
Hunter Avenged

City Light Shifters (Stand Alone)

Stolen Surrender

A Cumberpatch Cove Mystery

Death and Doubloons
Sabers, Sails, and Murder
Cauldrons and Corpses
Pets, Paws, and Poisons
Paints and Poltergeists

St. Claire Witches

Hexed by Fire
Spelled With Charms

CHAPTER ONE

Fall had officially arrived in Cumberpatch Cove, and so had the bewitching season.

In a community where anything paranormal was highly supported, the locals were gearing up for the arrival of Halloween. It was hard not to experience a little holiday exhilaration as I drove through town on my way to Evelyn Fulbright's coastal home.

Most of the houses and lawns had been decorated to celebrate the annual event. Even the trees lining the streets were prepared for the festivities. The ones whose branches weren't yet bare displayed vibrant orange, yellow, and red leaves.

The two-lane road that wound its way along the bay and overlooked the ocean was sparsely populated. The breathtaking landscape made up for the lack of homes adorned with decorations. I didn't get out that way very often, but I always enjoyed the drive when I did.

After slowing the car to make the turn onto the long graveled driveway leading up to Evelyn's place, I stopped to gawk at all the decorations. "Wow, do you think she went a little crazy this year?" I asked Grams, my grandmother on my father's side, who'd accompanied me and was sitting in the passenger seat, her dark cinnamon eyes even wider than mine.

When it came to Halloween, Evelyn had to be one of the holiday's biggest promoters. Besides holding a huge invitation-only party in her home every year, she'd also urged the city council to sponsor a haunted house.

The number of tourists who'd drive long distances to pay for a tour always amazed me. The place wasn't really a house, nor was it haunted. It was actually an old warehouse building on the outskirts of town that the council had converted to use for various events throughout the year. And when it came to having events, Cumberpatch was well-known for celebrating a plethora of them.

Numerous festivities meant numerous committees, which my mother Caroline continually volunteered me for. Not that I'd ever complain, especially when helping meant bringing a large amount of business to the Mysterious Baubles, my family's shop.

Since our activities were diverse, my parents insisted we carry a wide selection of items, including souvenirs, pirate paraphernalia, and my mother's special herbal remedies. Thanks to my father and his obsession with the supernatural, we even had several aisles dedicated to paranormal items. The things on those shelves that I found odd and sometimes scary were always popular with our customers.

Selling items wasn't the only thing our shop offered. For as long as I could remember, Grams made sure everyone knew she had dreams filled with premonitions and warnings about the future. She enjoyed adding a melodramatic flair to every story she told. It was probably why the tarot readings she offered at the shop were so popular.

Evelyn was an avid enthusiast, even more so after her husband Daniel passed away five years ago. When she was too busy to visit the shop for her readings, Grams made trips to see her.

A last-minute call to reschedule a reading was the reason for our current excursion, that and the two large cardboard boxes filled with the supplies she'd ordered from our shop for her upcoming Halloween party. Supplies my grandmother had graciously, and without asking my permission first, volunteered me to help deliver.

Grams giggled and pressed her face closer to the window. "There must be more decorations because last year I remember being able to see part of her lawn."

"Now that you mention it, I think you're right." I pressed on the accelerator, moving slowly to get a better view of the displays. It appeared as if Evelyn had found a holiday catalog and ordered all the items on every page. I'd seen some of the stuff in previous years, like the groups of lighted plastic pumpkins with hay bales as backdrops.

Evelyn had two life-sized witches and a scarecrow sitting together on an extended bench. A ghost the size of a hulking football player hovered between two trees, the air keeping it afloat supplied by a compressor.

Grams was right. If there was any dead grass underneath the elaborate displays, it was difficult to see.

Evelyn, or maybe Gary, the guy who maintained her property, had taken the time to string blinking lights with alternating orange and black bulbs around the posts supporting the canopy over her single-step porch. Her party was less than a week away, and with the number of decorations she'd displayed in her yard, I could only imagine what the inside of her house looked like.

Although I enjoyed helping Evelyn out and participating in the celebration, I'd never been much of a believer in the supernatural. Up until recently, I was the type of person who needed to see something for it to be real. I hadn't seen anything closely resembling the paranormal and refused to admit it even existed. At least not until a surprise birthday present from my father, Jonathan Spencer, had zapped me with extraordinary powers and introduced me to the world of spirits. Ones that only I could see and converse with.

After parking my car next to Evelyn's near the front of her white two-story house, I glanced at the door leading into the main foyer. It was partially open, and dead leaves carried by the breeze littered the few ceramic tiles I could see of the entryway's floor. "Grams." I touched her arm to pull her attention away from unsnapping her seat belt. "Does Evelyn normally leave her front door open like that?"

Grams paused to look up. "That's strange. I know she was expecting us, but she's never left the door open for any of my other visits. Maybe she stepped outside and forgot to close it." She shrugged and released her belt.

My grandmother might not be concerned, but I certainly was. Something was wrong; I could feel it, and so could every nerve in my body. They were pulsing with dread by the time we got out of the car.

I hoped my senses were mistaken, yet urgency drew me toward the door. I ignored the boxes we'd brought for Evelyn in the trunk and headed for the house. I could always retrieve them later once I'd confirmed that everything inside was okay.

The wind picked up, chilling the air. It swirled around me, seeped through my jacket, and made me shiver. Maine had been experiencing cooler days for weeks now. It wouldn't be long before the weather got colder and our occasional rain showers transformed into snow flurries.

Evelyn might be nearing sixty, but her memory was sharper than some adults half her age, and I'd never witnessed any signs of forgetfulness. With each step, I contemplated reasonable explanations of why the door would be open. Reasons that didn't involve anything suspicious or dangerous. "Why don't you wait here, and I'll check it out first." I gripped the strap of my purse tighter and took another step toward the entrance.

For an older woman, my grandmother could move fast. I hadn't realized she was so close until she latched on to my coat sleeve and made me jump. "You didn't seriously think I'd let my only granddaughter go in there by herself, did you?"

"So, are you saying if you had more than one granddaughter, you'd listen to me and wait by the car?" Stress and fear had a tendency to bring out my sarcasm.

She harrumphed and urged me to keep moving. I reached the opening first, but only by inches. I'd been raised with manners, and bursting into the foyer to discover that nothing was wrong might be construed as impolite. I decided that knocking first, then bursting inside would cover any social improprieties as well as any breaking and entering laws.

I reached for the knocker, then pulled back my hand when the red eyes of the gargoyle head started to glow. "What the…?"

"Amazing detail, don't you think?" Grams asked. "Evelyn had it installed a couple of months ago."

I couldn't argue that the detail was great, but amazing wasn't even close to the word I would've used to describe the gruesomely life-like thing. "Sure, I guess." I remained a foot away in case the knocker was programmed to do more than glow, then stuck out my arm and rapped on the door.

Seconds passed without an answer, so I called Evelyn's name. When that didn't work, I got a little bolder and pushed on the door eliciting a long, drawn-out creak. Besides making me shudder, the noise reminded me of every scary movie I'd ever watched where the heroine decided it was a good idea to enter a creepy old mansion.

Logically, I knew the house was old, and the noises were the result of settling. The hairs rising along my spine disagreed, and I wished I'd grabbed more than my purse to brandish as a weapon before heading inside.

As I'd suspected, the Halloween decorations hadn't stopped outside. Cobwebs and dangling spiders adorned the foyer. Beyond that was a massive room with stairs running along both sides of the wall and joining toward the middle when they reached the second floor. Typically, I'd pause to appreciate the beautifully handcrafted railings and the view of treetops that could be seen through the floor-length windows running along the wall on the upper floor. I was more worried about finding the place's owner, so admiring would have to wait.

Bubbling noises drew my attention to the right, where a large black and tarnished cauldron with orange smoke pouring over the metal edge sat on the floor. I wasn't an expert, but the pot looked authentic. If the burning logs underneath hadn't been fake, I'd have questioned whether or not Evelyn had recently taken up witchcraft.

"Evelyn," my grandmother called out, concern lacing her voice. "Are you here? It's Grams and Rylee."

As if in reply, a heavy thud echoed from somewhere in the house. I didn't think the hairs on my neck could stand any straighter. Nor did I realize how sharp my grandmother's fingernails were until she tightened her grip on my arm.

"Do you think that was her?" I asked since Grams had been in the house way more times than I had.

"I don't think so," Grams's voice came out raspy. She pointed toward the cauldron, or rather what was lying on the floor behind it.

I stared at the pair of dark leather shoes with square gold buckles, sitting with the back of the heels on the floor, exposing soles worn from extended use. Seeing the shoes didn't bother me. It was the legs covered with orange-and-black-striped stockings that were sticking out of them that had me shuddering and gasping, "Oh no."

I pried Grams's hand from my arm, then circled to the other side of the pot. Evelyn was sprawled on her side, the hem of her black dress bunched around her knees. She wasn't moving, and it didn't look like she was breathing. Wondering if she was alive and how she'd ended up on the floor outweighed any curiosity I had about why she was dressed in a witch's costume.

It didn't take much guessing to know from the odd way Evelyn's body was positioned that there was a good chance she wasn't going to be getting up any time soon. Probably not ever.

Just to be thorough and make sure I'd assumed correctly, I squatted next to her back and pressed my fingertips against her throat, checking for a pulse. Her skin still held some warmth, but I couldn't find a trace of life in her vein.

"Anything?" Grams asked, kneeling down beside me.

I didn't see any blood, so whether or not the cause of her death was natural, accidental, or intentional was hard to deduce. Seeing her body positioned close to the bottom of the stairs suggested her death might have been the result of a fall.

Since Grams and I had no medical certification or any kind of forensic training, figuring out how she ended up here was something the police would have to determine.

"No, I'm pretty sure she's…" Grams seemed to be handling the situation better than I'd expected, but I still found it hard to tell her out loud that her friend was dead.

"What's this?" Grams asked, leaning forward to see whatever Evelyn had clutched to her chest.

"Don't touch anything," I said too late to stop her from tugging on the object.

"Why not?" She sat back on her haunches, her glare jumping from the urn belonging to Daniel Fulbright to me. "Don't you think we should put it back where it belongs?"

The last time I'd seen his final resting place, the golden container mounted on a square wooden box had been displayed on the mantle above the fireplace in Evelyn's library. The room was down the hallway on the left and quite a distance from where she was lying. Why Daniel wasn't in his 'special place' seemed strange. Evelyn protectively clutching his urn seemed even stranger.

"No, I don't think we should put it back." I took Grams's free hand and helped her to her feet. "For all we know, this could be a crime scene. We need to leave the place the way we found it and call the police."

I'd watched enough mystery shows on television to know the police would check the urn's metal surface for fingerprints, which now contained several of my grandmother's. Unless I wanted her to become their main suspect, I'd need to mention how they got there when local law enforcement arrived.

"If Evelyn was here, I know she'd tell us to put Daniel back where he belongs." Grams wrapped her arms around the urn, and defiantly stuck out her lower lip.

Stubbornness ran in my family. Mentioning the irony of the situation wouldn't do me any good, but pointing out the obvious, on the other hand, might work in my favor. "Well, she's not here, so we can't ask her." I wiggled my finger at Evelyn, groaning after I realized I was standing next to a dead body arguing about the ashes of another deceased person when I should be dragging Grams back outside and making that much-needed call to the police.

"Are you sure?" Grams asked.

I quickly ran through the denial levels in my head, trying to determine which one was currently motivating my grandmother. It wasn't until I noticed the mischievous glint in her eyes and had the urn thrust at me that I realized grief had nothing to do with what she was after.

The instant the urn touched my skin, the cold metal warmed, and an electrical shock passed through my fingertips, zipped through my hands, and radiated along my arms all the way to my elbows. The only thing that kept me from tossing Daniel's remains into the air was the thought of seeing his ashes scattered across the tiles.

The jolt I received hurt, but it was nowhere near the level of pain I'd received when I'd handled the spirit seeker. After a single touch from that magical object, I'd been engulfed in blue tendrils and zapped into unconsciousness. When I'd awakened from the terrible experience, I could see spirits.

My new powers might attract spirits, but they also came with rules. Luckily, being bombarded by all the undead in town wasn't one of them. The magic I'd received enabled me to see, or rather help, one ghost find their way to the afterlife at a time.

The first ghost I'd seen was my friend Jessica who'd been murdered in the cemetery where she worked as a tour guide. My second was with Martin Cumberpatch, the not so famous pirate our town was named after. During that encounter, I discovered that touching an object—in his case, a cursed saber—could also release a spirit.

As much as I would've liked to return to my old life where I never interacted with anything paranormal, I'd learned from Joyce and Edith Haverston, the sisters who owned the Classic Broom, that getting rid of my newly discovered abilities was impossible. Since they had connections to the witching community in Cumberpatch—something I'd also recently learned existed—I had no reason to think they weren't telling me the truth.

It had taken me a while to adjust to the whole ghost whisperer thing, the title my best friend's Shawna and Jade had given my new abilities. It didn't mean I planned to go around touching old objects or people's personal possessions to find out if there was a spirit attached. But if one happened to make an appearance, I planned to do my best to help them.

Considering the tingle was quickly dissipating, I decided to be thankful I was still conscious. Even so, it did not excuse the members of my family from continually trying to short-circuit me.

"What the heck, Grams?" I snarled through gritted teeth and carefully set the urn, which now contained my fingerprints as well, back on the floor next to Evelyn's body.

I didn't have a problem admitting I was an amateur when it came to understanding all the rules about conversing with spirits. I'd heard ghosts didn't move on after their deaths if they had unfinished business often enough to do a little research. After surfing online and stopping by the local library a few times, I'd discovered that murder was the main reason spirits refused to leave.

Evelyn had recently died, but I'd received the electrical shock from Daniel's urn. A ghost was going to appear. I just didn't know how long it would take or who it would be: Evelyn or Daniel.

CHAPTER TWO

Under any other circumstances, dealing with Evelyn's body would have been a priority. But this situation wasn't one I encountered every day, and thanks to my grandmother, it was now complicated by an impending visit from a spirit.

"Did it work?" Grams asked, then glanced around expectantly.

"I'm not sure. It doesn't always happen right away." Scolding, even throttling my grandmother seemed appropriate, yet I found it hard to do either when she sounded so hopeful. "We'll give it a couple more minutes, and if nothing happens, then we call the police, *agreed?*" We'd already tampered with the crime scene. I didn't want to explain why we took so long to report the death after finding the body to our list of transgressions.

"Fine." I did my best to ignore the dejection lacing my grandmother's voice.

I was about to suggest that Grams and I wait for something to happen outside when the room suddenly filled with cold air.

"Can you feel that?" Grams shivered and pulled the front of her coat against her chest.

Experiencing a drop in temperature was an occurrence that always preceded the arrival of a ghost. A shimmering blue silhouette of a person appeared at the bottom of the staircase on the right. It flickered several times before manifesting into Evelyn. She was wearing the same witch's costume we'd found her in, only this one had the traditional pointed hat to go along with it.

"Rylee, when did you get here?" Evelyn asked, confused. "My hearing must be worse than I thought; otherwise, I would've heard you and Grams come in."

"Hey, Evelyn, I'm sure your hearing's fine," I said to alert Grams to her presence. Judging by her wide-toothed grin, she was delighted with the news.

"We do have a small problem to discuss." Okay, it was a huge problem, one I didn't think Evelyn had quite figured out yet.

Blurting out the bad news or asking a bunch of questions before she fully understood what happened might cause her to disappear. From what I'd learned, new ghosts weren't immediately equipped to deal with their predicament. Poofing out when stressed or startled could be troublesome. I didn't want to be the cause of either for Evelyn.

Thankfully, Grams had heard enough of my one-sided conversations with previous spirits to grasp my intentions and remain quiet.

"What kind of problem?" Evelyn asked. "Maybe I can help."

"Um, Evelyn, do you know what happened before we got here?" I slowly swept my hand toward the body on the floor.

She blinked several times, then leaned forward to get a closer look. "Is that…me?" she gulped, then held up her hands, twisting them from palm up to palm down as if seeing her translucent glow for the first time.

I nodded. "Yeah." I wanted to console her but knew my hand would only pass through her shoulder and feel as if I'd stuck it in a freezer.

It didn't take long for her confusion to pass, and her eyes to widen. "Are you saying I'm dead?"

"I'm afraid so." I released the breath I was holding when she didn't disappear.

She frowned and glanced at Grams. "Maybe we should do a reading just to be sure."

I rubbed my forehead and clamped my mouth shut before I could ask Evelyn what part of being dead she didn't understand. Of the two women who'd been friends for as long as I could remember, I'd never been able to decide which one possessed the highest amount of peculiar behaviors. I figured it was a tie most of the time, but Evelyn's request had quickly earned her the lead over my grandmother.

"Does she know how she ended up on the floor?" Grams asked, saving me the trouble of turning down Evelyn's request and getting her to focus on the current situation. I was also glad she'd given up on asking about whether or not we should put Daniel's urn back in the library.

Evelyn slapped her hands on her hips, then pinned Grams with a scathing glare. "You do know I'm standing right here and can answer questions for myself, don't you?"

"Evelyn, she can't see or hear you," I said. It was a good thing the two women weren't able to communicate or argue with each other. I wasn't in the mood to act as a referee.

"But you can... How is that possible?" Evelyn asked.

"It's a long story, one I'll be more than happy to share with you later. Right now, I need to know what happened." I thought back to when Jessica had first appeared and how she'd had problems with her memory. "Whatever you can remember would be great."

"Let's see." Evelyn tapped her chin, then glanced upward. "I was headed down the stairs when I thought I heard a noise coming from the hallway." Her smile faded into a grimace. "When I went back up to investigate, someone stepped out of the shadows. And they…" Her breath hitched, and her shimmer started to flicker. "They tried to grab me."

"It's okay," I used a soothing voice, urging her to calm down. "Take your time."

Once she solidified to her complete ghostly form again, I asked, "Can you remember how you ended up down here?" Doubts were high that it wasn't the result of a fall or that it had been an accident. I was leaning toward the attacker pushing her. Now that I was focused on how she'd died, I realized I'd been so distracted I hadn't considered that the killer might still be lurking around somewhere.

Would staying inside put Grams and me in any danger? The door leading into the room on the right was closed. Other than the loud thump I'd heard when we'd first arrived, I hadn't seen anything out of the ordinary move. Going outside sounded like a good plan, and I would have suggested it if I hadn't been afraid of spooking Evelyn and losing out on important information.

"This person who stepped out of the shadows," I reiterated for Grams's benefit. "Did you see who it was or get a good look at them?"

"No, they were covered in black and had some kind of mask on their face." Evelyn dropped her chin and patted her neck. "Oh, no, they took my necklace." Anger pushed her voice higher. "It was handcrafted and a gift from Daniel."

I turned to Grams and repeated everything Evelyn had shared so far.

"Was it the one shaped like a key with a skull on the end of it?" Grams asked.

"Yes," Evelyn sobbed.

I nodded in answer to Grams's question. The piece of jewelry had a distinct design, and I couldn't remember a

Halloween season that I hadn't seen Evelyn wearing it. "Was it valuable?" I asked.

"Not in the way you might think," Evelyn said.

Rather than get her to explain her confusing statement, I bobbed my head in answer to Grams's inquiring gaze.

"Why would someone want the necklace?" Grams paced a few steps. "And why would they push her down the stairs to get it."

Apparently, I wasn't the only one who'd made assumptions about how Evelyn had ended up next to the cauldron.

"Oh my." Evelyn wrung her hands. "Kevin is going to be so upset when he arrives."

I'd only met her nephew once, and it was during last year's party. His side of the family lived in Boston. He'd seemed like a nice guy, and from what Grams told me, he visited often and took good care of his aunt when he was here.

Grams had mentioned more than once how she wished Kevin would move here, so Evelyn wouldn't have to live in her big house alone. Giving Evelyn's body a quick glance, I now knew why she'd been so concerned.

"About what?" I asked since Evelyn had made it sound like her death wasn't what would be troubling Kevin.

"He was going to help me start decorating this afternoon for the party."

I wasn't sure what she thought still needed to be done. The place looked pretty inundated with decorations to me. "Considering what's happened, maybe we should worry about decorations later." I didn't have the heart to tell her the party would most likely be canceled. A murder had a way of dampening festivities. I glanced at Grams for support, bracing for an argument, and glad when I didn't get one.

"Rylee's right. We really do need to call the police." By call, my grandmother meant Logan Prescott. The handsome police detective and I had been dating steadily for almost a month now. A dead body, specifically Jessica's, had been how we'd met. It seemed to be an ongoing occurrence during our short relationship, and I knew he wasn't going to be happy when I told him I'd found another one.

The last corpse belonged to Jake Durant. Jade, Shawna, and I had discovered the man bobbing in the water next to my Uncle Max's boat, the *Buccaneer's Delight,* with a saber running through his chest. A saber that happened to belong to my uncle and made him the primary suspect until my friends and I discovered the real killer.

My relationship with Logan was new, and I hadn't told him about my ghost seeing abilities yet. Not because I wanted to keep secrets from him, but because I'd initially thought, hoped, prayed, and wished that the magic would go away. When that didn't happen, I wanted to make sure he could deal with my family's eccentricities first. There was no point in sharing something personal and not common knowledge with a guy if he wasn't going to be sticking around.

Surprisingly, Logan got along great with everyone, including Grams. What shocked me the most was the lengthy discussions he had with my father about his paranormal adventures. Some of the stories my dad told about visiting haunted houses over the years, including the ones he'd dragged me along to explore, could be lengthy.

None of the tales contained sightings of actual supernatural phenomenon, but Logan listened intently and always seemed interested.

Inevitable as telling Logan was, I'd planned to wait until my next ghostly encounter before discussing it with him. Putting it off any longer wouldn't be possible since he'd most likely be the one investigating.

From the moment I'd met Logan, he'd been adamant about me not getting involved with his cases. Now that I had confirmation about the cause of Evelyn's death, the only way to help her to the afterlife was to find the person responsible. I hoped once Logan knew about my abilities, he might be a little less stringent about his rule. Maybe even be more understanding and willing to lend me his help.

Delusional thinking and procrastination weren't going to prevent the inescapable, so I lifted the flap on my purse and pulled out my phone.

"You need to make sure they call Kevin and tell him what happened," Evelyn said, then did a little spin as if searching for something. "And someone needs to find Brutus." She pressed a hand to her chest. "You don't think whoever did this to me hurt my poor baby as well, do you?"

Poor baby? "Who is…" I groaned, hating that she'd disappeared before I could finish asking my question.

"What did she say?" Grams asked.

"We need to make sure someone calls Kevin." I swiped through my cell's contact list until I found Logan's number. "She also said we need to find someone named Brutus before she poofed out. Do you know who he is and why Evelyn would be so worried about him?"

Grams chuckled, then smiled, which was way better than seeing the bleak expression she'd been wearing when we'd first found her friend's body. "Brutus is the dog Kevin got for her."

"Oh," I said unhappily. Brutus was the kind of name someone might give a large animal. A large animal with sharp teeth. I didn't know much about dogs or their specific breeds, but an image of the ones used to guard a junkyard flitted through my mind.

"I'll bet he's around here somewhere." Grams searched the floor in the same manner Evelyn had.

I snagged her coat sleeve when she started to walk away. "Where do you think you're going?"

"To look for Brutus."

I hadn't heard any barking since we'd arrived and wondered if Evelyn had been right, that the dog had suffered a similar fate. With the front door open, he'd more than likely slipped outside. If Brutus was still alive, and we did find him, I hoped he had a friendly disposition and didn't decide that Grams and I would make good chewy snacks. I also wasn't going to let my grandmother go wandering around by herself. Who knew what else she'd find?

"It can wait until I'm finished with my call."

"What are we going to do about Daniel?" Grams asked.

I glanced down at the urn. "Daniel's fine where he's at."

"You didn't ask Evelyn about him on purpose," Grams said, then stomped toward the door.

I followed behind her. "Finding out what happened to Evelyn had seemed a little more important at the time." Our talk about Daniel reminded me that I wanted to know why Evelyn was toting around his remains to begin with, something I planned to ask her the next time I saw her.

While Grams continued her huff all the way to my car, I stayed on the porch and tapped the number for Logan's personal cell number.

He answered on the second ring. "Hey, Rylee, is everything okay?"

I didn't make a habit of calling him during working hours, and since we hadn't scheduled a time for our next get together, the concern in his voice was understandable.

"Well, I have a bit of a problem," I said, biting my lip.

"Anything I can do to help?"

"Actually, it requires your expertise."

"Which particular talent are you referring to?" I knew he was smirking. I could hear it in his teasing voice.

If the situation wasn't serious, I would have enjoyed his playful banter. Closing my eyes and taking a deep breath, I said, "I'm calling to report a murder."

"You're kidding, right?" His groan was loud and over-exaggerated. I imagined him pinching the bridge of his nose, maybe even shaking his head.

"I wish I were."

It was amazing how quickly Logan's tone changed, and he shifted into his detective persona. "Okay, tell me where you are."

After reciting Evelyn's address, I asked, "Is there anything you want me to do?"

"Wait outside, and don't touch anything. I'll be there as fast as I can." He disconnected the call without asking for any more details, which I assumed he would obtain once he arrived.

"What did he say?" Grams asked.

I slipped the phone back into my purse and walked toward her. "He'll be here soon."

Grams and I had already come to a semi-agreement about the urn so repeating his instructions about not touching anything seemed moot. "Why don't you wait here, and I'll check behind the house for Brutus?" I had no idea what else I'd find during my search for the dog. Having to deal with losing a friend was bad enough. If the dog had a mishap with the killer and was now a carcass, I didn't want my grandmother to see it.

"Rylee," Grams placed her hand on my cheek. "I'm a lot tougher than I look. You don't need to protect me."

Times like this, when she showed an exceptional amount of perception, always made me wonder if she actually was gifted with psychic abilities. I placed my hand over hers. "Believe me, I know." Any other time, the words would have been spoken with teasing sarcasm. In this instance, they were given with love and admiration. Most of the time, her antics made me crazy, but she was still my grandmother, and I'd always care about her.

Grams straightened her shoulders. "Roy and Logan will do a good job, but I want you to know I'm going to help you find whoever did this to Evelyn."

My grandmother was one of the few people who shared my secret and knew I'd do everything I could to solve her friend's murder. Grams might be inclined to make things more difficult, but I wasn't about to tell her no.

I draped my arm across her shoulder. "You're a Spencer. I'd expect nothing less."

CHAPTER THREE

I knew Logan wasn't going to be happy with me for disregarding his instructions, but finding Brutus seemed like a good reason for not staying put. Choosing between him being irritated and dealing with Evelyn's frantic new spirit was easy. I chose the latter, then reached behind the seat to grab the spare leash I kept for my pet cat Barley. I'd inherited the Kurilian Bobtail from Jessica shortly after she'd been murdered and I could see her ghost.

Grams had reluctantly agreed to wait for the police to arrive and was sitting sideways in my car's passenger seat with her feet touching the ground. I hadn't been fooled by the sweet and innocent old lady smile she'd been wearing since we'd left Evelyn's house, so I made her promise not to go back inside. To say I had trust issues when it came to my grandmother staying put and avoiding trouble was an understatement.

After giving her one last glance, I headed for the back of the house on my quest to find Brutus. The decorations covering the front lawn ended near the corner of the building. The yard running along the house's side was landscaped with a mixture of grassy areas and flowerbeds extending to a heavily wooded area. The grass, slowly succumbing to the colder weather, was no longer a vibrant green.

Since I'd only been in Evelyn's house a few times, mostly at night to attend the yearly parties, I wasn't familiar with the rest of her property. I'd already decided to keep my search in the open areas near the house. If Brutus had decided to wander into the woods, then he was on his own until Logan got here.

Using the path built with reddish-brown bricks, I walked beside the building on my way to the back yard. Halfway to my destination, the blocks split into two paths. One continued straight, the other veered to the left and ended near a cottage nestled close to the tree line.

The place was a one-story miniature version of the main house with the same exterior paint and trim, less the elaborate awning near the door. It was rather adorable and I was curious to know if anyone lived there. I considered the possibility of Brutus heading in that direction but didn't see any signs of movement.

I might have investigated if thoughts of it being a great place for a killer to hide weren't coupled with my grandmother sneaking up on me. "That's where Gary lives, but I don't think he's around right now."

"Grams," I squealed and spun around. "What happened to waiting by the car for Logan?" Frustration quickly replaced fear but didn't do anything to slow the pounding in my chest.

I released the tight grip I had on Barley's leash, glad I hadn't overreacted and smacked her with it. "I'm pretty sure Roy and Logan will be upset when they can't find us?" Telling Logan about my spirit seeing ability was going to be difficult enough. I didn't want to explain how I'd accidentally attacked my grandmother while we were wandering the grounds instead of following his instructions.

Grams stubbornly stuck out her chin. "They were taking too long, so I changed my mind."

"Uh-huh." I could understand her losing patience after a half hour had passed, but I'd made the call less than ten minutes ago.

"Besides, I started thinking about who might want to hurt Evelyn. Then I started thinking about a killer being on the loose. Then I started thinking about you being back here all alone." Grams had traded in her purse for the folded umbrella I kept in the car and was tapping it against her thigh in preparation for an impending assault.

She made it sound like a serial murderer was running around attacking anyone who got in their path. "So, you decided to give him or her two targets instead of one." I turned and continued toward the back of the house.

She tsked and followed after me, muttering something about ungrateful grandchildren and how bad I'd feel if something happened and she hadn't been around to protect me.

I clamped my lips together so she wouldn't see my amused grin. The woman was incorrigible, and letting her know how touched I was by her concern would only encourage her more.

A few steps later, my thoughts returned to her comment about Gary. He was Evelyn's gardener and maintenance man. He'd worked for her for years, but I hadn't known he actually lived on the property. "How do you know Gary's not home?" I asked.

"Max told me Gary was helping out with the pumpkin patch today," Grams said.

During the fall and winter months, my uncle shut down his pirate tour business and did odd jobs around town to stay busy. Working at the large pumpkin patch near the outskirts of town happened to be one of them.

Now that Grams had reminded me about Gary living on the property, he'd become a person of interest in Evelyn's death. Finding out if he was really at the patch all morning would be easy enough to confirm by talking to my uncle.

Of course, I'd have to come up with a good excuse before asking. Max was shrewd and hadn't heard about my ghostly ability yet. He hadn't been happy the last time I'd done some sleuthing, even if it was his innocence I was trying to prove.

I stepped into the back yard and got a breathtaking view of the bay and the Beaumont Inn. "Wow, this is beautiful."

"Yeah," Grams said. "Too bad the Abbotts own the inn, though."

Her reference to the Abbotts was directed at the sisters, Serena and Lavender. Technically, Serena, the older of the two, had earned her position as half-owner when she'd married Colin Beaumont, the hottest catch when we were all in high school together. Colin's family had owned the place for years. Lavender also worked there and was a high-ranking employee with no real ownership rights.

When it came to the Abbotts, my grandmother rarely had anything pleasant to say. Something had happened years ago between Grams and their grandmother. Something that the members of my family were still trying to uncover.

Most of the time, Serena was tolerable. Lavender, on the other hand, was an insufferable nemesis who'd gone out of her way to torment me for as long as I could remember.

Regardless of the ownership, the bed-and-breakfast type inn and surrounding property were well-maintained and added a rustic look to the already enchanting view.

The air coming in from the ocean was cold, so the breeze on this side of the house was chillier and strong enough to lift strands of my brown hair off my shoulders. It was also a good motivator to hurry our task and return to the front of the building.

I was about to ask Grams if she had any idea where we should look for Brutus when I heard whimpering coming from our right. "Did you hear that?" I stopped and tilted my head in the direction of the noise.

"No, what did it sound like?" Grams raised the umbrella as if she planned to brandish it at anything that moved.

"Kind of like a frantic whining." My leash wouldn't do much good in a battle, but it didn't stop me from gripping it tighter as I crept forward.

Grams strained to listen, then pointed at a thick wall of bushes on the other side of a rectangular patio trimmed with the same bricks used in the walkway. "I think it's coming from over there."

I inched closer to a spot where dirt formed a small mound on the lawn near the edging that ran along the bushes. Once I got closer, I spotted a furry creature frantically digging near the exterior wall. "Is that Brutus?" The name didn't fit the white and tan ball of fluff that wasn't much bigger than the miniature schnauzer Jade's mom owned. I bet if we shaved off all his fur, he wouldn't be much larger than my cat either.

"Sure looks like him." Grams walked up next to me, making sure to avoid being hit by any flying debris. "Can you see what he's digging?"

"Not unless I go into the bushes after him." Which I had no interest in doing. Whatever Brutus was after had his full attention. He seemed utterly oblivious to our presence.

Until Barley came into my life, I'd never owned a pet and hadn't known the first thing about taking care of one. I might not be an expert, but I wasn't a novice either. I reached into my pocket where I kept a sealed bag of cat treats. I didn't think Brutus would mind that the tiny snacks were shaped like fish and not specifically designed for dogs.

I poured a few treats into my hand, then leaned forward and cooed, "Hey there, boy." Just because he was small didn't mean his teeth weren't sharp. I took a few cautious steps forward. "Look what I've got for you."

Brutus immediately stopped pawing and snapped his head in my direction. His growl was low, though not overly threatening.

I maintained my distance, then squatted on the ground and lowered my hand until it was closer to his eye level. If he ran, there was no way I'd be able to catch or find him if he decided to head for the trees. "Come on, you know you want these."

He inched toward me, stretching out his neck to sniff my fingertips with his cold, muddy nose. It took a few seconds for the dog to trust me enough to snarf the treats, then whimper and prance, expecting more.

"Looks like you made a friend," Grams said.

"Yeah, but don't tell Barley I gave away all his snacks," I giggled and emptied the remaining contents into my hand.

I waited for Brutus to start eating again before snagging his collar and snapping the end of the leash through the hook. After scratching the soft, fluffy fur on his head to get some of the dirt off, I got to my feet. "Come on, let's go see if Logan's arrived."

"Are you going to tell him about Evelyn…her spirit, I mean," Grams asked, pacing beside me.

"I don't think I have a choice, not if I want our relationship to continue." Which I did.

"If he can't accept you for the special person you are, then he doesn't deserve you." She patted me on the shoulder. "And if he thinks differently, I'll be happy to tell him otherwise."

Grams and her cohort Mattie, who owned the coffee shop across the street from our shop, had been playing matchmaker with me as their focal point for years. To hear she'd threaten Logan, even if it meant breaking us up, was a complete surprise. "Thanks, Grams, I appreciate the concern, but I'd rather handle this one myself."

"If you're sure." She raised a brow, then stopped when we'd reached the patio.

"I'm sure."

"Why don't we just cut through the house and save ourselves from walking all the way around?" Grams pressed down on the door handle. "Look, it's not locked."

"Why did the intruder risk being seen entering the front when they could have sneaked in through here?" I was still trying to come up with a satisfactory reason for the front door to be open when we'd arrived.

"They wouldn't," Grams said.

"Exactly." I snapped my fingers with my free hand. "Let's…" I didn't get a chance to tell her we should go around anyway.

"You weren't planning to go back inside after I specifically told you not to, were you?" Logan's deep voice reached us seconds before he did.

"No." Guilt laced my tone, and heat coated the skin from my throat to my cheeks. Then my stomach fluttered like it always did every time I saw him.

I preferred seeing him in jeans, but he looked good in the black casual pants he was wearing. He kept his hands tucked in the pockets of a tan suede jacket and narrowed his dark whiskey gaze. "Good, because I'd hate to have to take you both down to the station for breaking and entering."

Brutus was growling, and the number of times I could handle being startled in a day had reached its limit. Dealing with an unhappy boyfriend wasn't helping either. "Told you," I grumbled and shot an accusatory glare at Grams.

Grams had already closed and moved away from the door. After flashing me a smile that was anything but innocent, she scooped Brutus off the ground. "This is Evelyn's dog, and we were afraid something bad had happened to the poor little guy." She walked over to Logan and practically thrust the dog in his face daring him to be angry about our rescue.

The dog made happy whimpering noises and excitedly licked Logan's chin. If I didn't know any better, I would have bet my grandmother and Brutus had been practicing the cute puppy act for weeks.

CHAPTER FOUR

After using Brutus to pacify Logan's concerns about Grams and me wandering around Evelyn's property, she'd taken custody of the dog and was leading him around the house with Barley's leash. I was certain Logan had questions but other than asking my grandmother and me if we were all right, he hadn't said much.

By the time we'd reached the front of the building, there were two law enforcement vehicles parked behind my car on the circular drive. The medical examiner van had yet to arrive. The vehicle parked closest to us had the word SHERIFF emblazoned on the side in bold black letters. No doubt Logan had come with Roy, which meant his uncle was probably inside checking out the crime scene.

To confirm what I was thinking, Roy picked that moment to step out onto the porch. He and Logan were close to the same height, with similarities in their appearance. They both had the same defined jaw and whiskey-colored eyes. Where Logan's hair was dark, Roy's was a shade lighter and intermingled with silver.

After giving us an acknowledging nod, Roy glanced toward the patrol car and shouted, "Barnes, are you

29

coming with that tape?"

"Yes, sir," Elliott replied, then reached inside his vehicle and grabbed a yellow roll. On his way back to the house, he puffed out his chest as he strutted past us. His tall, lanky form wasn't muscled enough to fill out his uniform, so his belt always hung low on his narrow hips. "Afternoon, Abigail, Rylee."

Like me, Elliott was born in Cumberpatch. We'd known each other since high school. Any other time, even when he was on duty, he'd address my grandmother by her nickname like all my friends did. I knew his professional act was his way of trying to impress his boss and Logan.

"Elliott," Grams and I replied.

As soon as Elliott reached the porch, Roy walked over and put his hand on Grams's shoulder. "I'm so sorry about Evelyn. I know you two were close."

"Thanks, I'll miss her eventually," Grams said.

"Eventually, but she…" Roy stammered.

I aimed a warning glare at my grandmother. "I'm sure Grams is still in shock." And if she wasn't, she was going to be if she blabbed about Evelyn still being around.

Logan didn't say anything, but I knew by his inquisitive look that he wasn't buying my excuse, not after his recent puppy encounter with Grams and Brutus.

"Where'd you find the dog?" Roy squatted and held out his hand palm up so Brutus could sniff him.

"He belongs to Evelyn," Grams said. "We found him out back digging."

"He seemed pretty adamant about getting whatever was behind the bushes," I said.

"I can see that. Maybe he was trying to find a bone or something he'd buried earlier." Roy swiped at the smudge of dirt I'd missed on Brutus's nose. "What are you planning to do with him?"

I hadn't given it much thought but had a feeling Evelyn would be upset if I let the police take her pet. I couldn't tell Roy and Logan that I knew Kevin was due to arrive sometime today, not without explaining how I knew. "I guess he can come home with me for now."

I didn't think Barley, being a cat, would appreciate a dog for a house guest. Maybe keeping Brutus for a couple of days wouldn't be so bad. If it turned out I was wrong, I could always ask Shawna and Jade if they would look after him until I could talk to Kevin and see if he wanted to take the dog. Though we'd have to find out if their apartment complex allowed pets.

"I hate to ask but would you two mind answering a few questions?" Logan asked.

I rubbed my arms. The breeze had picked up again, and the cold had finally seeped through my jacket. "Would it be okay if we did it inside where it's warmer?"

"Sure, not a problem," Roy said as he turned to head for the house.

"Roy." Grams stopped him by placing her hand on his arm. "I'd rather not go back inside. If you don't mind, can we do the questioning in your car, preferably with the heater on?"

Gram's solemn expression could've won her an award. I knew she mourned her friend, but since she hadn't had a problem hovering around Evelyn's body earlier, I suspected the part about staying outside was feigned.

Knowing my grandmother, she wanted to keep Roy busy to give me a chance to talk to Logan privately about Evelyn. It was the reason I didn't let the sheriff see me roll my eyes.

"Here, why don't you take him with you?" Grams picked up Brutus and shoved him into my arms. She leaned closer and whispered, "You might need him to help smooth things over if a certain someone gets upset again."

I glanced at Logan, who was hiding a grin and pretending not to have heard what Grams had said. Brutus snuggled his cold nose against my neck. I didn't need any more distractions and handed him back to Grams. "I'll be fine, thanks."

"Come on," Roy said, motioning Grams toward his vehicle.

Logan walked up beside me. "We can stay out here if you'd rather."

"I'm good. Besides, there's something else I need to talk to you about."

"Should I be worried?" he asked.

Only if he had a thing against people who could see ghosts or had inadvertently tampered with his crime scene. "No, but I might consider making you promise not to get upset before I tell you." I released a nervous laugh.

"Would you mind waiting out here for the examiner?" Logan asked Elliott, who'd stopped stringing his yellow crime scene tape along the porch long enough for us to duck underneath.

"Not at all," Elliott said. "Do you want me to work crowd control as well?"

There wasn't anyone to monitor, but this was Cumberpatch, and gossip moved faster than a flame on a trail of gunpowder. Evelyn's isolated home could be seen from the Beaumont Inn. The police had no reason to be on the coastal road, but anyone who'd noticed their vehicles would be curious and want to investigate.

"You do that," Logan placed a hand on my back and urged me inside.

He'd transferred from a bigger city a little over a month ago and seemed to be acclimating to our community's idiosyncrasies without any difficulty. He stopped in the foyer and asked, "Are you sure you're okay with being back in here?"

I nodded. This was the third corpse I'd seen this year, and it was still unsettling. Even worse because I knew the victim and had really liked her.

I stared at the cauldron. From where we were standing, all I could see were Evelyn's shoes. Thankfully, she hadn't made a reappearance. With any luck, she wouldn't show up until I was done talking to Logan.

"There's a room over here we can use," Logan said after noticing the direction of my gaze. He seemed familiar enough with the rooms along the hallway and led me to Evelyn's library. Had he checked out the entire house when he'd first arrived and couldn't find Grams and me?

Two of the walls inside the room were lined with books. A bay window comprised most of the third, and a brick fireplace was centered on the fourth. "Why don't you tell me what happened from the time you arrived until the time you called me?" Logan asked after motioning me to take a seat on a sofa facing the fireplace.

I spent the next few minutes giving him the sequence of events, starting with the reason for our visit and ending with our search for Brutus.

"Is everything the way you found it?" Logan's tone suggested he already knew the answer to the question.

I didn't have to ask to know he was referring to Daniel's urn. Sitting by itself on the floor behind Evelyn's body must have appeared strange to someone who'd investigated numerous crime scenes. "Sort of."

"What do you mean sort of?" Logan's exasperated tone made me cringe.

"Well, Evelyn was holding the urn when we arrived, and Grams might have picked it up, then handed it to me."

"Might have?" Logan asked.

"Okay, did." I squirmed on my seat. "In my defense, I didn't let her put the urn back on the mantle where it belongs." I cast a glance at the empty space on the wooden shelf on the fireplace.

Though he was still frowning, he didn't seem nearly as upset as I'd expected. "Is that what you wanted to talk to me about?"

"Uh, no. When I touched the urn, I was able to see Evelyn's ghost." I'd planned to start at the beginning and incrementally tell him about my abilities, not blurt out my latest experience and shock him into silence. There was nothing like ripping an entire box of Band-Aids off at once to make a situation worse.

His dark eyes widened, and I could almost hear the thoughts zipping around in his head. I clutched the purse sitting on my lap, willing myself to remain quiet and wait for him to say something first.

"Are you telling me you can actually see spirits?" he asked.

"I can converse with them too." That didn't sound any more convincing than my first statement.

"Okay." He drew out the word and continued to eye me intently.

If this was going to end badly, I wanted to get it over with. After taking a deep breath, I asked, "Remember when we first met?"

"You mean when you ran me off the road?" Maybe it was my imagination, but I hoped I'd heard a hint of teasing in Logan's voice. "I do. Why?"

"Do you also remember how I'd mentioned Jessica's name before you ever told me she was the reason you were headed for the cemetery?"

"Yes," his voice deepened.

"Earlier that day, I'd received a birthday present from my father. Only it wasn't the kind of gift you'd normally expect to receive." Logan had interacted with my father enough times that I didn't need to explain about the abnormalities surrounding his gifts any further. "What I thought was an unusual box of chocolates turned out to be a spirit seeker."

One of Logan's brows lifted. "A spirit seeker?"

"It's an object that grants someone the ability to see ghosts." At the time, I was certain I'd been cursed by the darned thing. I could see the skepticism in Logan's gaze. He dealt with reality the way I used to, so I added, "I have it locked away in the storeroom at the shop if you ever want to see it."

When he didn't say anything, I continued, "Jessica's spirit appeared in the passenger seat of my car, and that's

34

why I swerved before you ended up in the ditch." I was in a hurry to get my story out, caught myself rambling, and paused to take another breath. "It's also how I knew she was the person who had been murdered."

"Rylee, I…"

I held up my hand. "Wait, there's more."

"I'm listening," he said.

I finished by giving him brief details about my encounter with Martin and his cursed saber. I then went on to tell him how my friends and I had been trying to help both ghosts move on to their afterlife, which was how we'd ended up helping solve their murders.

The last time I'd seen Martin and his dog Pete they'd been standing on the deck of his pirate ship. Martin's circumstances had been different. He'd been bound to his saber and had been in our realm for centuries. Even though I hadn't seen him since that night, I wasn't totally convinced either of them had moved on to the spirit realm.

And if I was right, and Logan and I were still together—possibly big if judging by his frown—then I didn't want Martin's existence to be a surprise.

"So, why are you just telling me about this now?" Logan crossed his arms. "Why not say something sooner?"

I hated being the one responsible for the disappointment I heard in his voice. "I know I probably should have, but I was a murder suspect in your first case, then my uncle was a suspect in the second. And, at the time Jessica and Martin moved on to the afterlife, we weren't actually dating." I really liked Logan, his intense detective side and all. But the last thing I needed in my life was a boyfriend who didn't believe me even if I was a little late in telling him the truth.

A woman's shriek sliced through the air, putting an end to our conversation.

"What the…" Logan jumped to his feet and raced from the room with me following close behind him.

A woman bearing the same facial features as Evelyn stood in the foyer with her hands on her hips. Her hair had been dyed a shade of black too dark for her pale complexion, which contrasted with the tan jacket and pale blue skirt she was wearing.

"What happened? Where's Evelyn?" She obviously hadn't gotten a glimpse of Evelyn's body yet. "Is she all right?"

Logan approached the frantic woman, doing his best to block her view in the process. "Excuse me, but you can't be in here."

Elliott flew through the open doorway a few seconds later. "Sorry, Logan. She got past me."

That was understandable. The woman was wider and must have weighed at least thirty more pounds than Elliott.

"I'll take it from here," Logan said, dismissing Elliott, then turning his attention back to the woman. "Now, would you mind telling me who you are?"

"I'm Lydia Fassbinder. My sister Evelyn lives here," she spouted the words as if they were meant to hold some importance.

"Well, Ms. Fassbinder, there's been an accident, and I need you to step back outside and let us do our job." Logan held out his arm in an attempt to get her to turn around.

"What kind of accident? Did something happen to Evelyn? Was she robbed?" Lydia took another step forward, craning her neck and trying to see around Logan.

"Lydia, maybe we should leave and go back to the inn," said a balding man who'd been quietly standing off to the side near the open doorway. Dressed in a heavy plaid sweater over a collared shirt, the man appeared thinner and a couple of inches taller than Lydia. He'd taken a few timid steps, then stopped to wring his hands.

Cumberpatch only had one inn, which meant they were staying next door. Evelyn's house was large and had plenty of room. It seemed strange that the couple wouldn't be staying with her instead.

"Not now, Harold." The warning glare Lydia directed at the man caused him to wince. "I'm not leaving until I find out what's going on here. I didn't drive all the way down the coast this morning to see Evelyn and attend her party this weekend just to be thrown out of her house."

I wasn't impressed with the way Lydia had spoken to Harold and couldn't resist prodding the nasty woman before Logan ushered her back outside to answer questions. "I thought Evelyn's sister lived in Boston."

The only sibling Evelyn ever talked about was her sister Charlotte who also happened to be Kevin's mother. I guessed Lydia's age to be around forty, so she had to be the youngest. I'd never heard Grams mention the woman before and wasn't sure if they even knew each other, a fact I had disproved a few seconds later when my grandmother appeared in the doorway carrying a squirming Brutus. "Lydia," Grams sneered as she strolled past her.

"Abigail," the disdain in Lydia's voice sounded mutual.

If Evelyn's sister was always this pushy and rude, I could see why Evelyn had never mentioned her. Brutus didn't seem to think much of her either. He'd been making growly noises ever since Grams carried him into the room.

Lydia dismissed my grandmother with an upturn of her nose, then continued speaking to me. "You must be thinking of Charlotte. She's our older sister." Lydia stuck out her narrow chin as if it should be common knowledge, and I'd somehow insulted her.

Cold air seeped through the open gap at the front of my jacket. It was the only warning I got before Evelyn appeared beside me. "Lydia always was overly dramatic even when we were children." She was still wearing her witch's costume, but her hair shimmered a brilliant purple, not blue like the rest of her body.

I pressed my lips together to keep from smirking. Those were details I wouldn't mind hearing but would have to wait until later. I hoped Evelyn didn't ask me any questions because I wouldn't be able to answer any of them. Grams and now Logan were the only two people in the room who knew I could talk to spirits. And so far, my grandmother was the only one who believed me.

"And who are you, anyway?" Lydia asked.

"I'm…"

"This is my granddaughter, Rylee." Grams inched protectively closer and returned Lydia's glare.

"Oh, I heard all about you," Lydia beamed. "You're supposed to be some kind of witch or something."

"I'm not a witch." Though the or something part had been accurate. If Lydia stayed at the Beaumont whenever she was in town, it wasn't hard to figure out who she'd gotten the information from.

I now understood Shawna's fetish for wishing she could transform people into frogs. If I could cast spells, I visualized what Lydia would look like if someone changed her into a large gray toad.

She swirled her finger between Grams and me. "I didn't know witchcraft ran in your family, Abigail."

"Lydia." Roy used his authoritative voice to interrupt her.

Besides growing up in Cumberpatch, Roy had been the sheriff for a long time. I didn't think there was anyone in town that he didn't know.

"Yes, Roy." Lydia's snide tone dulled when she answered, though not by much.

Roy gave Lydia his back. "Rylee, maybe you should take Grams home now."

I didn't like where Logan and I had left things in our conversation, but now wasn't the time to finish the discussion.

"Go ahead," Logan said. "We can talk again later."

Pressure tightened my chest. Logan's emotions were hard to read, and I had no way of knowing what would be said when we resumed our conversation.

"Sure." I hooked my arm through Grams's, then with a tip of my head in Evelyn's general direction, headed out the door.

CHAPTER FIVE

After thanking me for finding Brutus, Evelyn announced that she wouldn't be riding back to Mysterious Baubles with Grams and me. She wanted to remain at her place so she could hear what her obnoxious and untrustworthy sister had to say to Roy and Logan. The words used to describe Lydia had been Evelyn's, but I didn't have a problem agreeing.

It was a good thing Evelyn had stayed behind because I'd spent most of the drive focused on the conversation I'd had with Logan while Grams cooed and consoled Brutus about losing his owner.

We'd been at Evelyn's most of the afternoon, and it was nearing closing time when we reached the shop. As soon as the bell above the door tinkled, my mother glanced up from the shelf she was stocking with Halloween scented candles shaped like goblins. "How did it go at Evelyn's?"

"You mean besides finding a dead body?" Grams stalked to the back of the store.

Thankfully, I didn't see any customers. Besides Jade, my parents were the only ones in the shop.

Jade was standing behind a display case. She was

wearing a slimming black dress with a wide teal belt, which happened to be her favorite color. After securing a spider web to the wall, she propped her elbows on the counter. "Oooh, did Evelyn get some new decorations?"

"You could say that, but it's not what Grams is talking about," I said.

"It's not?" Jade asked, her blue eyes sparkling with interest.

Grams waved her hand through the air. "Evelyn's dead." She dropped her purse on the counter next to the cash register, the thump emphasizing her dramatic proclamation. "So, we have a new ghost to help and another murder to solve."

I was too shocked to speak. Within seconds, my grandmother had gone from being a doggy grief counselor to a determined sleuth. I groaned and tugged on Brutus's leash, then headed down the nearest aisle with him prancing beside me. Every few seconds, the furry ball of fluff stopped to sniff something he'd found on the floor.

My mother, who I'd inherited my medium brown hair and not so tall height from, placed a hand on her chest. "That's horrible. What happened? I thought you were just going out to her place to do a tarot reading and drop off supplies."

Grams had a reputation for overexaggerating situations. I wasn't surprised to see my mother narrow her gaze as if she thought my grandmother had made up the story.

Since this was one of those rare occasions when my grandmother told the truth, I did what any good granddaughter would do and defended her. "Evelyn was already dead when we got there."

My father was standing on a ladder in the corner, no longer concentrating on hanging his favorite skeleton with glowing eyes from the ceiling. He glanced over his shoulder and asked, "Mom, what are you talking about?" He'd obviously ignored Grams's dramatic entrance and most of our conversation. He left the skeleton to dangle by one arm and climbed down the steps to pin me with an accusing glare. "Wait, did you say something about a new ghost?"

I, in turn, glared at my grandmother for blabbing about my secret. Since he hadn't said anything right away, I'd hoped he'd missed that part of Grams's announcement as well.

"Uh-oh," Jade muttered, then clamped a hand over her mouth.

My parents had been traveling for the last few months and had left me in charge of the shop. They'd only been back a couple of weeks to take a break and attend Evelyn's party. Since I'd been ghost-free for nearly a month, I hadn't bothered telling either of them about the new ability I'd gotten from the gift my father had shipped to me at the beginning of summer.

"Rylee, is there something you want to tell me?" He crossed his arms and continued to give me his full attention. "I thought you said the spirit seeker didn't work, that you couldn't see any ghosts."

Being an adult didn't stop me from feeling like a child when under the scrutiny of one or both of my parents. I struggled to come up with a reasonable explanation that would appease my father. I'd stopped moving the second he started questioning me. I was standing in the middle of the herbal aisle, too far from the front door to grab Brutus and dash back outside. "Technically, I was telling the truth. When you called to ask me whether or not I'd seen any ghosts, I really hadn't."

"So, now that we've established that you can see ghosts, how many have you seen exactly?" Leave it to my mother to pick up on the small details.

"You mean counting today?" I asked apprehensively.

I received a stern yes, followed by a pause, then the word "please" from my mother.

"Three."

Grams hurried over and draped her arm across my

shoulder. "In all fairness, you can't be angry at Rylee. That so-called present you sent her almost killed her." She used her protective motherly tone, which worked to have everyone in the room but me cringing. "The first time she saw a ghost, you two were on a cruise, and *we* couldn't reach you. The second time you were on vacation in Las Vegas. You've talked about going for years, and there was no way we were going to call you and risk ruining your trip." She puffed out an indignant breath.

At the rate my secret about having paranormal abilities was being shared, I wondered if it wouldn't be easier to have Troy Duncan, the only reporter for the Swashbuckler Gazette, interview me and post an article in his family's newspaper. At least then, everyone in town would know the truth, and Lavender wouldn't get any enjoyment out of telling people I was a witch. It was something I'd need to consider, but not until after I'd finished helping Evelyn.

I'm sure my family would support the idea if it brought in more business. Then again, I wasn't sure I was ready to go public and would need to give the ramifications further thought. "I'm sorry I didn't say anything, but can we worry about filling in the details later?"

When I was first able to see spirits, I'd hoped the magic was temporary and would fade away on its own and had been careful who I told about it. The fewer people who knew I could converse with Evelyn, the easier it would be to search for clues. It would prevent whoever was responsible from discovering that my friends and I had more information than the police and were also looking for them. The last thing I wanted to do was put the lives of those I cared about in danger, not to mention my own.

"I need you all to promise you won't be telling, mentioning, discussing, or eluding to my new"—I made quote marks with my fingers—"gift with anyone." My determined gaze landed on each of them in turn, saving Grams for last since she was the one I worried about the most.

"Not even, Max?" my father pouted. He and his brother were close. They shared the same kind of relationship I had with Jade and Shawna.

"I think it's something I should tell him myself if that's okay with you," I said.

Jade walked over to join the group. I could always count on her to show support by coming up with a way to change the subject. As soon as she spotted Brutus, she asked, "Who's this cute little thing?" She knelt down and unhooked the leash, then giggled when he attacked her hand with his tongue. "When did you decide to get another pet?"

"I didn't. This is Evelyn's dog, Brutus. I volunteered to take care of him until her nephew gets into town and will hopefully give him a home."

Now that we were on the topic of pets, I realized mine was missing. "Wait a minute, where's Barley?"

"Shawna has him in the back office trying on his new Halloween costume." Jade stood up, bringing Brutus along with her.

I should have known after my friend had dressed him up for the pirate festival that she wouldn't let a holiday pass without putting Barley in another costume.

"Don't worry, you'll love it," Jade said after interpreting my scowl correctly.

"I'd like to get back to the topic of solving a murder," my mother said. "If you can see another ghost, then where exactly did you find Evelyn's body?"

"Evelyn's dead?" Shawna's disbelieving voice filtered from the entrance of the hallway leading to the back of the building. "No way." She strolled into the room carrying Barley.

She was wearing her work uniform and must have already finished the lunch shift at the Cumberpatch Cove Cantina. It was hard not to notice the blue streaks running through her curly light brown hair, a definite sign she and Nate were still dating.

Her colorful stripes had gone from a vibrant purple at the beginning of summer to the shade she now wore once she'd discovered it was his favorite color. Her relationship with guys rarely spanned more than a few months. So far, the bet Jade and I had about how long their courtship would last seemed to be failing. At the most, we agreed they'd make it until New Year's Eve.

"Where did you find Evelyn?" Shawna asked. "What happened to her? And, more importantly, does this mean she's not going to have her party this weekend?"

"Shawna," Jade and I said at the same time.

"What? It's a legitimate question." She placed Barley in my arms so I could get a better look at his costume.

"A unicorn, seriously." I ran my fingertips along the iridescent gold horn between the horse-shaped ears in the center of the white furry cap fastened to his head. His gray and black-striped fur stuck out in all directions, making him look like a wild cat, minus a tail—a characteristic of his breed. Correction, he looked like a unicorn version of a fuzzy furball.

"Cute, right?" Shawna asked.

"Okay, I'll admit it's adorable." Since Barley's purr had reached the level of loud rumble, I assumed he didn't mind his new outfit. It also meant he hadn't seen Brutus, either that or he was content to ignore him.

"Can we get back to the ghost part of the conversation?" my father asked.

"Are you saying Evelyn's a ghost?" Shawna grinned and gave the room a thorough perusing.

It wasn't like Shawna could actually catch a glimmer of the ghosts, so I didn't know why she always glanced around at the mention of a visit. If I could read her mind, which I'd been thankful on more than one occasion that I couldn't, I'd bet she was already devising ideas for our next covert sleuthing mission.

"She is, so we need to help Rylee find out who killed her," Grams stated emphatically. It appeared volunteering wasn't an option. After Grams issued her statement, she glared at everyone in the room but me daring them to refuse.

"Can you explain what happened to Evelyn and why Rylee has to be the one to find the person responsible for her death?" my mother asked.

Being concerned about her only child heading into a dangerous situation was understandable.

"Evelyn won't be able to move on unless she gets resolution." I didn't want to worry my mother further by relaying the time constraint issues Edith and Joyce had told me about. The ones that would trap Evelyn in our realm if her killer wasn't found.

Grams didn't seem to have the same concerns about my mother as I did. "You don't want Rylee to be stuck with Evelyn's ghost forever, do you?" she asked as she stepped around me and went to lock the front door.

My mother scowled. "No, of course not."

I glanced at my watch. It was already a quarter after five, fifteen minutes past regular store hours. "Do you need help closing up?" I'd had an exhausting day but would stick around if my parents needed me to.

"No, we've got it covered," my father said. "I am curious about one thing?"

"Only one?" I imagined he had a lot of questions since he'd just heard his daughter could talk to ghosts."

"Does Evelyn look like a zombie?" The way my father curled his fingers, straightened his arms, and rocked side to side had everyone giggling.

When my mother's laughter subsided, she said, "Jonathan, there are days when I worry about your abnormal interest in the undead."

"Rylee," Evelyn's appearance made me jump. "Did you tell your father I looked like a zombie?" She stared down her front, then strained to see her back.

"No, Evelyn, I didn't tell my father you looked like a zombie." The mention of her name drew everyone's attention. I bobbed my head to let them know she was with us. "He got the information from the object that zapped me and gave me the power to see spirits." I glanced at my father. "Other than an ethereal blue glow, new spirits look the same way they did in real life."

In case Evelyn wasn't aware and might take offense, I left out the part about them changing their appearance or that she was wearing a new outfit. I couldn't decide if it was supposed to be a princess costume or a fairy godmother. If it was the latter, the only thing missing was the magic wand.

"Well, that's too bad," my father said, earning him a thump on the arm from Grams. "Evelyn might be dead, but she can still hear you."

"Grams is right." I hooked my thumb in her direction. "So, if you have any questions, please feel free to direct them to her, and I will relay her answers." Grams, Shawna, and Jade already knew what to expect. But since this was the first time my parents had been around during one of my ghostly encounters, I decided it would be easier to fill them in on how things worked.

"Better yet," I said. "Why don't we finish this conversation at my place? I can order some pizzas while you finish shutting down for the night." My home happened to be the apartment above the shop. It wasn't large, but it had plenty of room to accommodate all of us.

Jessica told me Barley thought he was a dog, something I'd witnessed on numerous occasions. As soon as I mentioned pizza, he started to squirm and flex his claws to get down.

Brutus had been exploring the shop ever since Jade removed his borrowed leash. I'd been so preoccupied with our discussion I'd forgotten all about him until I set Barley on the floor. The shop was my cat's domain, and it didn't take him long to sniff out and find the miniature intruder. Rather than the hissing and growling I'd expected, I got to watch a faux unicorn tussle with a small ball of fur.

"Barley, Brutus, stop that." My mother had an authoritative voice that seemed to work on small creatures the same way it did on children. Both animals stopped, then immediately parked their backsides on the floor as if they'd been issued a command to sit.

"That was awesome," Shawna said.

"It really was," I agreed. "I don't suppose you'd be willing to spend the night on my couch to make sure these two continue to behave, would you?" I knew what the answer would be before I asked, but figured I'd try anyway.

CHAPTER SIX

A half hour after I left the shop to take Barley and Brutus back to my apartment, some of the group showed up to join me. Max had called and needed my parents to help with a project. That left Grams, Shawna, Jade, and I to devise a plan to help Evelyn.

My father had wanted to see a ghost his entire life. Not being able to hang out with Evelyn had to be a huge disappointment. I knew I should feel guilty, but I was glad my parents wouldn't be involved while discussing possible suspects and devising a plan. It was going to be difficult enough keeping my grandmother from causing trouble.

We all settled into the living room with the newly arrived pizzas and the ample supply of wine coolers Grams had brought with her. The living room and kitchen were basically one long room. It made seeing and talking to Evelyn easier. She'd chosen to sit on one of my dinette chairs and looked quite regal with her wide ankle-length skirt billowing out around her.

As usual, Barley, less his new costume, had found a spot under the table near our feet where he could wait for any morsels that landed on the floor. Brutus didn't use a subtle approach. He jumped up on the sofa and settled between Jade and Grams. So far, the two animals seemed to get along reasonably well. I didn't think they'd ever become best friends, but at least they were no longer wrestling with each other.

"It would sure be nice if you'd seen the person's face," Shawna spoke in Evelyn's general direction, then stacked the three pizza boxes full of pepperoni with extra cheese on my coffee table.

I'd already shared the details I'd obtained from Evelyn earlier in the day with my friends.

"Evelyn," I said, setting out paper plates along with the napkins that came with the delivery. "I think the best place to start would be to find out if there's anything else you can remember."

When I'd first questioned Evelyn about her demise, she'd been too worried about Kevin and finding Brutus to thoroughly discuss all the details. There was also a chance she'd had time to recall something she'd forgotten. "Would you mind telling us everything that happened before Grams and I arrived?" I flashed her an encouraging smile, then slipped a slice of pizza on a plate.

Evelyn rested her arm on the table and tapped the surface. In her ghostly form, her fingernails didn't make any noise. "My housekeeper Vivian came early to clean. I opened the door to let Brutus outside to take care of business, then remembered I hadn't moved Daniel back to the library like I do every morning."

I repeated what she'd said. "Move Daniel from where?" I asked after noting the quizzical looks on everyone's faces.

"My bedroom." Evelyn held up a hand. "And before you ask, the answer is no, I don't sleep with my husband's ashes. I keep his urn in my room at night because it's comforting to have him nearby."

I wasn't about to judge, not when I had a father obsessed with anything paranormal and a grandmother who consistently told everyone she received psychic premonitions via her dreams. The one recollection I'd heard the most involved visits from my great-great-uncle Howard, who liked to come back as various types of animals, most of them rodents.

Supposedly, he only made an appearance when a member of our family needed help. The last so-called reincarnation was a mouse who kept stealing morsels from my muffins when I'd helped Jessica. He'd disappeared shortly after her spirit departed, and I hadn't seen the mouse since.

The downside to being able to talk to ghosts was that no one else could hear them. It drained my patience to repeat the spirit's side of the discussion. Luckily, my friends had gotten good at interpreting what was said from hearing my side of the conversation. In this instance, I repeated what Evelyn said verbatim.

Grams didn't seem surprised by the information and continued to sip from her cooler. Jade coughed after nearly choking on the bite of food she'd swallowed. Shawna made an agreeable noise, then asked, "Does Vivian always come early to clean the house?"

"No, she normally comes after lunch," Evelyn said.

"If she usually cleans in the afternoon, why the different time?" I asked.

"She'd called me the day before and asked if she could switch since she was also working part-time at the pumpkin patch this year," Evelyn said.

"Did you actually see Vivian leave before you were shoved...I mean had your mishap," Shawna corrected after Jade, Grams, and I glared at her.

"No, I don't think so." Evelyn fluffed the portion of her skirt covering her knees. "I remember her telling me she was getting ready to leave right before I went to get Daniel, but I didn't actually see her go."

"I'd say that makes Vivian a suspect, don't you?" Shawna paused with a slice inches from her mouth. "There's a reason they always say the butler did it." Unable to hear Evelyn's horrified gasp, she continued to shove pizza in her mouth.

"You are aware there is a huge difference between a butler and a part-time housekeeper, right?" Jade asked.

I reached for the pen and pad I'd set on the table. "Not that I think Vivian did it, but I think she should go on the list until we know for sure," I said for Evelyn's benefit. At the top of the sheet, I wrote the word "suspects", then scribbled Vivian's name right below it.

"Didn't you say the front door was open when you got there?" Shawna asked. "Did you guys see anybody suspicious running from the house? Or a getaway vehicle parked closeby?"

"No, there wasn't anyone around," I said. "Evelyn's car was the only one parked in the driveway when we arrived. I don't remember seeing any vehicles parked along the main road, either." I glanced at Grams. "Do you?"

"Not that I recall, but I wasn't paying much attention." Grams used setting her empty bottle on the table as a distraction to slip Brutus a piece of pepperoni.

"Maybe Gary saw someone, though I don't know if he was still home by then," Evelyn said.

"Evelyn suggests we speak with Gary," I told the group.

"Oooh, then you need to write his name down too." Shawna wiggled her finger at the notepad. "According to the guide, gardeners, groundskeepers, handymen and women also qualify as people of interest."

"What guide?" I asked as I added Gary's name to our list.

"The Universal Whodunit Guide, of course." Shawna snorted indignantly. "I can't believe you didn't know that."

"You've been spending a lot of time on the Internet again, haven't you?" Jade asked, moving her plate to keep Brutus from snatching remnants of her pizza.

"Hey, it's a great way to learn things," Shawna said.

"Evelyn, is there anything else you can remember?"

Grams asked, directing the conversation toward a safer subject.

"Did I mention I'd heard noises right before...I was attacked?" Evelyn asked.

"You did," I said. "Can you describe the noises? Were they thumps? Creaks? Doors slamming?"

"Creaks definitely creaks." Evelyn wrinkled her nose.

"Was this the first time you heard creaks in that hallway?" I asked.

"No, I also heard them a few weeks ago, but it was later in the day," Evelyn said. "I thought it might be Daniel trying to reach out to me from the other side. That's why I wanted Grams to do a reading."

Tarot cards were supposed to help people gain insight into their past, present, and future, not make a direct connection to the spirit world. It was too late to tell Evelyn she should have sent for a psychic. If Grams had known what Evelyn had in mind, I'm sure she would have recommended her friend Nadine for the task.

After rubbing my forehead, I relayed all the information to my friends, excluding the part about Daniel since I already knew it wasn't him.

"If Rylee's handsome detective was here, he'd probably be asking if Evelyn had any enemies." Shawna set her empty plate on the table, then leaned forward and scratched Barley's head. Since she'd failed to share any morsels with him, he rolled on his back and latched onto her hand. "Hey, play nice." She scolded as she extracted his claws from her skin.

I hadn't had a chance to tell my friends about my conversation with Logan. A talk I'd been trying hard not to think about since I was afraid it might put an end to our short relationship.

"How could I possibly have any enemies?" Evelyn crossed her arms and glared at Shawna. "I'm an old lady who lives or rather lived with her dog."

"That would be a no," I said, pretty sure if my friend

continued to upset Evelyn she might find herself with an enemy.

Evelyn had stopped giving Shawna the evil eye long enough to glance in my direction. "Since we're on the topic of the police, do you know if they talked to Kevin yet?"

"Didn't Kevin show up when you stayed behind to listen in on Roy's conversation with Lydia and Harold?" I asked.

"No, I tried to follow my sister when they were finished and ended up at the shop with you."

"What did Evelyn say?" Grams asked after taking a sip from her cooler.

"Evelyn's worried about Kevin since he didn't show up while she was at her house," I said.

"Who's Kevin?" Shawna asked.

"It's Evelyn's nephew," Jade said. "We met him at the party last year, remember?"

"Oh yeah, he's the guy you thought was good…" After being smacked in the cheek with a flying piece of pepperoni, Shawna's shock didn't last long. She picked up the piece of meat, intent on flinging it back at Jade.

I furrowed my brows. "Hey, no food fights in the house."

"Fine." Shawna tossed it on her plate instead.

"Anyway, I'm sure Kevin's fine," I said for Evelyn's benefit. "Maybe he got a late start." I didn't want to upset her further by telling her that Logan might consider Kevin a suspect until he verified his alibi.

Just because Grams and I didn't see a vehicle near the cottage didn't mean Evelyn's nephew hadn't been there and wasn't the killer. He visited her often enough to know the town and the property quite well.

Grams figured out that I was trying to console her friend and added, "Or maybe he got stuck in heavy traffic. Cumberpatch does get a lot of tourists this time of year."

"You're probably right." Evelyn didn't sound like we'd

reassured her any. "Maybe I'll just go check for myself." It was the last thing she said before vanishing.

"Evelyn disappeared again," I said.

"What? Why?" Grams asked.

"She went to look for Kevin." Though with the problems she was having reaching her intended destinations, I worried that she wouldn't be successful.

"Maybe we should call it a night. Without Evelyn to answer any more of our questions, anything we come up with now would only be speculation." Jade pushed out of her seat, then gathered the dirty paper plates off the table and headed for the kitchen trash can.

Grams glanced at the watch on her wrist, then got up to help with the cleaning. "I would have to agree. It's getting late, and I have to work in the morning."

By the time we'd finished, and everyone left, I was exhausted, and I didn't think I'd be able to retain any more facts. I perused the two names on my page of suspects, then as an afterthought, added Lydia, Harold, and Kevin. Of the three, Lydia and Harold had already given Logan their alibi, but because family members usually had the strongest motives I wasn't ready to exclude them yet.

I had no idea what the killer's motive had been, but maybe by tomorrow, and after another chat with my friends, I'd figure it out.

CHAPTER SEVEN

I was glad volunteering to take in another pet was going to be temporary. Barley might have accepted Brutus after their initial confrontation at the shop, but territory lines were drawn when the three of us got to my apartment. I didn't have time for a trip to the pet store, so Brutus had to share Barley's cat food. An event that worked much better once I'd set the bowls on opposite sides of the room.

Bedtime hadn't worked out quite as well. Barley hadn't been happy to share his bed and human with a fuzzball that took forever to find a place to sleep on my comforter. Eventually, he calmed down, and I got in a few hours of sleep.

Grams wasn't the only one scheduled to work. My parents might be taking a respite from traveling, but I was still in charge of running the shop, which meant ordering inventory and dealing with the stack of papers on my desk.

After securing leashes to collars, I scooped Barley into my arms and semi-pulled and walked Brutus down the stairs to the back entrance of the store. Once inside, I released them again, hoping any damage they caused racing down the aisles would be minimal.

Since they'd retired, my parents had gotten in the habit of arriving mid-morning. Today, they sauntered in shortly after Grams unlocked the front door for business.

"Well," my father said, excitedly twisting his hands together. "Is Evelyn here?" He moved his head from left to right to glimpse around the room.

My mother didn't show the same enthusiasm, but I could tell she was anxious to hear what I had to say.

"Good morning to you too, dad," I said, slipping the cash tray into the register and closing the drawer. "I haven't seen her yet today."

"Why not?" His smile faded. "I thought haunting meant all the time."

"I'm afraid it doesn't work that way, and I can't control when she appears."

"Can you at least tell us what Evelyn had to say last night?" my mother asked.

Whatever project Uncle Max and my parents had worked on must have been important; otherwise, my father would have found a way to get out of it.

I spent the next fifteen minutes sharing what my friends and I had learned, with Grams interjecting her own personal insights about the information. By the time the bell above the front door tinkled and three women wearing matching Cumberpatch Cove T-shirts over long-sleeved sweatshirts walked into the shop, I was mentally exhausted.

"Oh, my goodness, look at all the wonderful decorations," one of them said after glancing around the room. "I told you this was going to be a great place to shop."

"Good day, ladies," my father said as he strolled over to them. "Is there anything I can help you with?"

My grandmother was an excellent salesperson, and she'd taught my father well. Within minutes he'd charmed our newest customers and was leading them down an aisle to the opposite side of the store.

Not long after that, the front door opened again, and Jade and Shawna sauntered into the shop.

"Hey, everyone," Shawna said, turning to me. "Are we still on for our excursion this morning?"

Getting pumpkins to carve and display on the sidewalk outside the shop had become a yearly ritual. The tradition had evolved into a competition to see who came up with the best creations between all the owners who had businesses on Swashbuckler Blvd. It was one of the few times Grams and her friend Mattie, who owned the coffee shop across the street, competed instead of conspiring with each other.

"Absolutely." My enthusiasm drew a curious look from my mother and grandmother. Since Vivian was at the top of my suspect list, the outing would allow me to chat with her if she happened to be working. Besides confirming whether or not the reason she'd given Evelyn for modifying her cleaning schedule had been the truth, Vivian might be able to provide another clue.

Before I could usher my friends to the area behind the store where I parked my car, the cordless phone mounted on the wall behind the counter containing the cash register started to ring. My mother was the closest, so she answered by reciting our shop's name, followed by a polite "This is Caroline".

She listened intently before saying, "Yes, she is. May I ask who's calling?" Another pause. "Can you hold for a moment?" She placed her hand over the mouthpiece and in a whisper asked, "Were you expecting a call from a guy named Kevin?" Then quickly added in a stern tone, "You didn't break up with Logan, did you?"

My parents adored Logan, so any kind of breakup would automatically be my fault. "No." I wiggled my fingers so she'd stop holding the phone hostage. "This is Rylee," I said once I'd obtained custody of the phone.

"Hey, Rylee," a male voice responded. "This is Kevin Patterson. I don't know if you remember me, but I'm

Evelyn's nephew." His voice was deep and pleasant but held a hint of sadness when he said his aunt's name.

"I do, and I'm so sorry about what happened."

"Thank you, me too."

After a few seconds of silence passed, I asked, "Is there something I can do for you?"

"Oh, yeah, sorry. I went by the police station this morning and spoke with Detective Prescott. He told me you were taking care of Brutus. I was wondering if we could meet somewhere so I can pick him up."

I had no way of knowing whether or not Kevin was the person responsible for his aunt's demise. According to Evelyn, her nephew was supposed to arrive yesterday. There might be a good reason why he hadn't, but until I knew for sure, I preferred having a discussion with him in a public place. If it weren't for my family and the possibility of an interrogation, I would've suggested he come to the shop.

"Do you know where the pumpkin patch is?" The patch was an open location and seemed like a better choice. I could drop off Brutus, talk to Vivian, and if I was lucky, Gary might be there too, and I could question him about Evelyn as well.

"I do," he said.

"I'm headed that way now. Would you be able to meet me out front in a half hour?" If he couldn't, I'd have to come up with a backup plan.

"It might take me a little longer to get there, but that works fine for me," Kevin said.

"Great, I'll see you then." I placed the phone back in its receiver and turned around to find my parents standing on the opposite side of the display case. They were practically leaning on the counter, not bothering to hide the fact that they'd been eavesdropping. Shawna, Jade, and Grams were standing behind them, trying their hardest not to giggle.

"If you weren't able to hear the other side of my phone

call clearly, that was Evelyn's nephew, and we're"—I pointed at Jade and Shawna—"meeting him at the patch so he can pick up Brutus."

It was hard to tell which of my parents released the loudest relieved sigh. Grams was notorious for sharing information at the most inopportune times. Not to be spiteful, at least not often, but because she believed whatever she knew would be useful. In case she decided now would be a good time to tell my parents about my conversation with Logan yesterday, one that could potentially impact things in a bad way, I decided it was time to go.

After a quick scan of the aisles, I found Barley showing Brutus how to knock bottles of herbs off the bottom shelf. I scurried over to the naughty animals, then knelt to give my cat a scratch behind the ears before snatching Brutus off the floor.

"It's time to go," I called to my friends, then just as quickly, with the dog precariously tucked under my arm, I headed for the back of the shop.

CHAPTER EIGHT

Once my friends and I were on the road and headed to the pumpkin patch, Brutus curled up on Jade's lap and slept for most of the trip. I assumed Jade had acquired her animal calming skills from growing up with her mom's excitable schnauzer.

If I was making a comparison, I'd say Shawna was a lot like Brutus, always busy, with no fear of getting into trouble or considering the possible consequences. It was probably why Jade was able to live with Shawna without wanting to strangle her daily.

With the additional tourist traffic, the drive to Dingerson's farm where the pumpkin patch was located took most of the thirty minutes I'd given Kevin for our meeting. The farm's owner had cordoned off a field to use for parking. We'd gotten lucky and found a spot close to the entrance. At the rate people were arriving, I estimated that finding decent places to park would be more difficult in another hour.

"Do either of you recall what Kevin looks like?" I asked as I climbed out of the car. The one and only time I'd met him had been at Evelyn's Halloween party. He'd been wearing an impressive vampire costume and had white paint covering his face. The only defining features I remembered were his tall height, defined jaw, and the red lines drawn near the ends of his lips that closely resembled blood.

"You mean besides a broad set of shoulders, silky light brown hair, and sparkling amber eyes? Sure, I have a vague recollection of what he looks like," Jade said, flashing Shawna and me a wide grin.

"I'm glad to hear he didn't leave an impression." Shawna winked and wiggled her brows at me.

"Me too," I laughed.

Jade was picky about the men she dated, and I was glad to see her show some interest in a guy. I was also protective of my friend and didn't want to see her get hurt, or worse, end up dead because she got involved with a potential killer.

"Good looking or not, I think he should be treated like any other suspect until we know for sure he didn't off his aunt," Shawna said what I'd been thinking.

Jade stopped walking and glared at Shawna and me. "You don't seriously think he had anything to do with his aunt's death, do you?"

"We have no way of knowing." When Jade's hands went to her hips, bracing for an argument, I added, "At least not yet."

"I'm with Rylee," Shawna said. "In most domestic murder cases, a family member is usually the person responsible."

"Well," Jade huffed. "Now's your chance to find out which of us is right because there he is."

The guy Jade had directed our attention to waved, then strolled toward us. She'd been right about the broad shoulders and the color of his eyes. Eyes that lit up the instant he recognized Jade. Without the painted face, the familial connection to Evelyn was easy to see.

Like Jade, Kevin also had good taste in fashion and was dressed in dark casual pants and a wool sweater over a button-down shirt. As soon as Brutus spotted him, he whined and tugged on his leash, trying to get away from Jade.

"Hey there, boy. I missed you too," Kevin said, then knelt to pet the fluff on Brutus's head. The dog raised up on his hind legs, pawed Kevin's chest, and covered his chin with wet doggy kisses.

Once Kevin was back on his feet, he smiled at my friend and asked, "Jade, right?" It appeared the interest Jade had been doing her best to conceal wasn't one-sided. His gaze remained locked with hers as if Shawna and I didn't exist.

"You remembered." Jade blushed like a teenager, something I'd rarely witnessed.

Kevin finally glanced in my direction. "And you're, Rylee." His gaze moved to my left. "And Shawna?"

"Yes." I nodded. He was definitely scoring points for remembering our names, especially with my friends.

"Thanks for meeting me and taking care of Brutus." Kevin grinned, showing off his dimples.

"It was no problem." Though I was pretty sure Barley would disagree with me.

"I understand you and Abigail were the ones who found my aunt." The sadness I'd detected earlier had returned to his voice.

"I'm really sorry about Evelyn. She was such a nice lady." In my mind, I tried to focus on the shimmering blue image I had of the older woman, not the one of her contorted body splayed on the floor.

"You mentioned that you met with the police this morning. Do they have any idea what happened?" Evelyn hadn't reappeared since the night before, but I didn't think they'd solved the case already. Though it was possible.

"The meeting with Detective Prescott was more like an interrogation," Kevin said. "I got the impression he thought I might have had something to do with my aunt's death."

"Maybe Rylee can put in a good word for you since Logan is her boyfriend," Shawna said.

I couldn't tell if the shock on Kevin's face meant he was considering the option or wary of my connection with a member of the police force. "Shawna," I snapped.

"What? It's not like it's a secret or anything," she huffed.

"Talking to the detective won't be necessary." Kevin cleared his throat. "But I did have another reason for wanting to meet with you."

He'd kept me from throttling my friend, so I mentally gave him points for diplomacy. "You did?"

"Yes, after I ran into Edith and Joyce Haverston yesterday afternoon I..."

"You were in town?" I interrupted before hearing his reason. When I'd talked to Evelyn, she'd made it sound as if he'd be traveling and wouldn't be arriving until later in the day. I couldn't say anything about it to Kevin, not without explaining how I'd gotten the information.

"I wanted to surprise Evelyn," Kevin said, his cheeks flushing.

If, by surprise, he meant helping her down the stairs, then he'd been successful. I wasn't going to accuse him of harming his aunt, not without evidence, but Shawna might.

"Surprise?" Jade asked, using a less intrusive approach.

"I planned to tell her I was relocating my art gallery to Cumberpatch."

"That's so sweet." Jade was practically gushing.

"It would have been if I'd gotten the chance to tell her." Kevin glanced down at Brutus, who was happily sniffing the ground near his feet.

"So, did you find a place, and are you moving here?" Shawna asked.

I didn't know if her prying was because of Jade's interest in the guy or if she was trying to confirm his alibi.

"Yes, I met with Grace Dunleavy yesterday afternoon to look at some buildings I could rent. It took longer than

I'd anticipated to find the right location and do the paperwork." Kevin's jaw muscle tightened. "By the time I got to my aunt's place, it was too late."

Grace was a local realtor. It would be easy enough to confirm Kevin's explanation with a phone call to the chatty woman. Now that I was fairly certain I could scratch Kevin off my list, I was more than a little curious to hear what the Haverston sisters had to say. "You mentioned talking to Edith and Joyce."

"I've had strange conversations with them before, but Edith said something that didn't make any sense," Kevin said.

I held back a snort. Lately, every interaction I'd had with the sisters ended with an odd piece of advice. "What did she say?"

"That you'd be able to help my aunt in a way the police couldn't."

"Did she happen to say how I could do that specifically?" I tried to remember if I'd asked her and Joyce not to go around telling people about my ghost seeing ability or if I'd assumed they would be discreet. So far, they had.

"No, and when I asked her if she could be more forthcoming, she would only tell me that you could *see* things others couldn't. She'd really stressed the seeing part." He glanced at the ground as if searching for the right words. After a few seconds, he raised his gaze again. "You're not psychic, are you?"

I wasn't thrilled the sisters had suggested Kevin talk to me, but I was relieved they hadn't given him any specific details.

"Why, do you believe in the paranormal?" I asked, unsure if he was teasing.

"You can't visit Cumberpatch without embracing the possibility…at least a little. Evelyn believed, and I suppose that helped me keep an open mind. That and the occasional cuff to the back of the head when I was younger," Kevin said with a wink.

He was personable like Evelyn. I could see why the two of them got along so well.

Kevin glanced at the groups of people walking past us. "I should let you get going before all the good pumpkins are taken." He bent over and picked up the dog. "Thanks again for taking care of Brutus." He started to unhook Barley's leash from Brutus's collar.

"That's okay. The leash is a spare. You can return it to me later." Kevin looked like a strong guy, but I worried about the dog's tendency to squirm. If Brutus got away from him and wandered off, who knew how long it would take to find the dog again.

"I appreciate it," Kevin said, then set Brutus back on the ground. "If you need to reach me, I'll be staying at the Beaumont."

"Why not at Evelyn's house," I asked, wondering if going inside would be difficult for him after what happened.

"I'm afraid it's still a crime scene," Kevin said.

"Sorry, I forgot about that."

"It's okay; your detective friend assured me it would only be there a few more days, a week at the most." Kevin smiled at Jade. "It was nice seeing you again. Maybe once I get settled, we can get a coffee or something."

"I'd like that," Jade said, the color on her cheeks growing brighter than her lipstick.

After Kevin was out of earshot, Jade nudged my shoulder. "Don't you think you should have told him about being able to see Evelyn?"

"Evelyn hasn't been around all morning," I said, urging my friends toward the entrance to the patch. "What if he wanted me to prove I could talk to her and asked me questions only she could answer?"

My friends and I had a longstanding agreement we'd made back in our younger days. We didn't share each other's secrets, not without permission, and especially not with our families. I could count on either of them not to tell Kevin I could see spirits without getting my approval first.

"Good point, but knowing she's still around might have made him feel better," Jade said, opening her purse to pull out money to pay the entrance fee.

"I think the only thing that's going to help anyone feel better is finding out who wanted her dead," Shawna said, reaching in her coat pocket to do the same.

"Once we find Max, would you mind picking out the pumpkins without me?" I asked.

"Why, what are you going to do?" Jade asked.

"First, I'm going to have a chat with my uncle." I raised my brows, cluing them in to the topic without saying it out loud. My father could only be trusted to keep a secret so long. Eventually, and more by accident, he'd end up saying something to Max.

Shawna snapped her fingers. "Oh, yeah, right?"

"And after you have your talk?" Jade asked.

"I'm going to see if Vivian is working and discreetly ask her some questions." I was afraid if we showed up as a group, Vivian might be reluctant to share information.

After getting in line and paying for our tickets, we followed a group of people onto a large field where pallets had been placed in rows and covered with various-sized pumpkins.

My uncle was a tall, broad-chested man with a boisterous laugh, and finding him was easy. Instead of a spooky costume like some of the other employees were wearing, Max was dressed like a pirate, one of the uniforms he wore when he ran his tours. I waited for him to finish loading a wheelbarrow with pumpkins for one of his customers before walking up to him. "Morning, Max," I said, giving him a hug.

"Ladies." He smiled at my friends, then me. "How's my favorite niece and her partners in crime doing?"

"I'm your only niece," I laughed. "But we're all doing

fine."

Shawna and Jade confirmed my assessment by answering with a "yep" and "yes", respectfully, of their own.

"I take it you're here to get some pumpkins for the carving contest," Max said.

"We are." I waited for Jade and Shawna to start perusing the vast selection on a nearby pallet. "Actually, there's something I need to talk to you about first." I tipped my head, motioning him away from other shoppers.

"Sounds serious. Is everything all right?"

"Yeah, it's just…" Explaining should be getting easier since I'd done it enough in the last couple of days, but it hadn't. "Remember that day on your boat when you thought I shot you and Jake with the water cannons?"

"Yes, why?" Max asked.

"It was really Martin Cumberpatch's ghost who pulled the trigger."

"Rylee." He used his no-nonsense tone and folded his arms across his chest. "I don't have…"

"Wait, there's more." I rushed to share the same details I'd given my parents, ending with how Grams had purposely gotten me to summon Evelyn's spirit.

"Do your parents know?" he asked.

"I told them yesterday."

"That explains why your father was acting so strange last night. He must have been ecstatic when you told him." He placed his hand on my shoulder. "You know you could have told me sooner." He sounded more disappointed than upset.

"I know, and I'm sorry. It's just that I was hoping the powers would fade, and my life would go back to being normal." Or normalish, considering the oddities of my family.

He scratched his beard. "I assume this is something you're trying to keep a secret."

"At least for now." I offered him a weak smile.

"Was that all or was there something else you were after?" My uncle and my father were a lot alike, but Max was way more perceptive.

I stuck my hands in my jacket pockets. "I don't suppose you could tell me if Vivian Trumbell is working today, could you?"

"I take it you want to talk to her because she was Evelyn's housekeeper, right?" he asked.

"Maybe." I bit my lower lip, feigning innocence.

He shook his head. "I'd be wasting my breath by telling you not to investigate, wouldn't I?"

I shrugged. "It's either that or doom poor Evelyn to this realm and haunting me forever."

A chuckle rumbled from his chest. "Well, we definitely can't have that. You'll find Vivian over in the petting zoo. She's the one wearing the Little Bo Peep costume."

"Thanks, Max, you're the best uncle ever." I threw my arms around his neck, which was difficult since he was several inches taller than me.

The petting zoo was a small barn sitting on one end of a large pen comprised of a four-foot-high fence. It was designed to entertain children. The animals housed inside the pen appeared friendly and included three goats, a miniature donkey, and a baby lama. With the purchase of a paper cup filled with pellets, anyone could feed the creatures. Children lined the outside of the fence while their parents stood close by to help them.

In the past, I'd found it amusing to watch the young ones interact with the animals. Today, however, I was on a mission. I'd never met Vivian and had no idea what she looked like. It helped that she was the only one in the group wearing a costume and handing out pellets.

"Are you Vivian?" I asked as soon as I got closer.

She looked up after handing a boy around the age of seven a disposable cup decorated with a Halloween theme. "I am, and who are you?"

"I'm Rylee Spencer."

Vivian's bright smile faded. "You're Abigail's granddaughter." She took a step back and stared at me as if I was going to cast magic, and she'd be the recipient. "I heard you're the one who found Evelyn. Is it true? Is she really dead?"

"Yes, to both." I glanced around, noting that it wouldn't be long before more children came asking for pellets. "I know you're busy, but I was hoping you could answer a couple of questions...about Evelyn. It would really mean a lot to Grams, I mean my grandmother."

News about me finding Evelyn had traveled faster than I thought. I knew if Logan and Roy had already questioned her they wouldn't have said anything. My choice for someone who had the information and was capable of spreading rumors would be Lydia. Although there was a chance Grams had already talked to Mattie, who was also notorious when it came to gossiping.

Vivian still seemed nervous and took a moment to ponder my request before answering, "Oh, sure, what did you want to know?"

"I understand you worked for Evelyn, that you were there yesterday morning."

"I was, but I didn't...I would never..." Vivian's rambling transformed into tearless sobs.

Unless she was an exceptional actress, her concern seemed genuine. "I was more interested in whether or not you've noticed anything strange lately, like creaking sounds?"

"Why would you ask me something like that?" Her defensive tone brought the sniffling to a stop.

Telling her I'd gotten the information from a ghost would only make things worse. "I'm only asking because Evelyn mentioned that she'd heard noises during one of her tarot readings with my grandmother."

"Oh." Vivian relaxed the tight grip she had on her blue hooped skirt. "I only clean a couple times a week. Evelyn's old house made noises, but I've never heard anything I thought was strange. Maybe you should ask Gary. He's worked for Evelyn a lot longer than I have."

"Is Gary here?" I hadn't seen him for quite some time and didn't think I'd recognize him if he was wearing a costume.

"No, he doesn't like to be around a lot of people and only helps with the setup," Vivian said.

"Excuse me." A little girl with blonde pigtails came up and tugged on Vivian's skirt. "A goat took my cup, and my mom said I should ask you to get it for me." She pointed at the brown and white goat with long floppy ears with a partially mangled cup hanging from its mouth.

Vivian scowled. "They really should put up a warning sign. Beatrice likes to chew on everything." She smiled down at the child who appeared to be on the verge of tears. "Come on, we'll get you a new cup."

After thanking Vivian for her help, I went in search of my friends. I was halfway to my destination when a child's squeal drew my attention. When I glanced over my shoulder to see the little girl happily running toward the fence with her new pellet-filled cup, I collided with the only person who could ruin my day.

"Why don't you watch where you're going?" Lavender smoothed the front of her jacket as if my bumping into her had somehow rumpled it.

"Sorry," I struggled to sound pleasant, which did nothing to remove the sneer from her face.

"Let me guess, you're here to get pumpkins so you can practice changing them into carriages?"

The flippant remark I was about to make never made it out of my mouth. Jade appeared next to me and said, "No, but you should see her transform people into animals." She draped her arm across my shoulder. "Would you like a demonstration? Black cats seem to be popular this time of year, but personally, I prefer lizards."

I'd seen Lavender stomp her feet before, but I didn't know she was capable of growling like a wild animal.

"Lizards, really?" I leaned my head against Jade's as we watched Lavender storm toward the parking lot.

"Hey, being four-legged and scaly doesn't mean they're not cute." Jade lowered her arm. "Besides, Shawna's not the only one with a maniacal sense of humor."

I laughed. "Speaking of our mischievous friend, where did you leave her, and should I be concerned?"

"Don't worry. She's helping Max load our pumpkins. Though the mention of a wheelbarrow race did come up in the conversation before I left."

CHAPTER NINE

Helping Evelyn was a priority, but there were other important things in my life that I couldn't neglect. Attending the town's annual haunted house with Shawna and Jade was one of them.

Apparently, it was high on Evelyn's must-do list as well. On our drive there, she appeared in the backseat of my car next to Shawna. My reaction to being startled after hearing Evelyn say my name during one of her unannounced visits had gotten a lot better. I didn't swerve all over the road or end up in a ditch.

"Hey, Evelyn," I said to let Jade and Shawna know she was traveling with us. Although, by the way Shawna was vigorously rubbing her arms from the chill, I felt certain she was close to saying something about it.

I glimpsed in the rearview mirror and noticed that Evelyn had switched costumes again and looked like a huge shimmering bumblebee. The fuzzy yellow ends of her antennas were the only parts of her outfit that weren't blue.

"I finally found Kevin," Evelyn said. "He's staying at the Beaumont because Roy still has my house cordoned off with tape." She pressed her lips into a thin line.

It was a good thing she had trouble finding locations and couldn't move objects. Otherwise, I feared the sheriff would have gotten a visit and seen some of his personal possessions flying around.

"I overheard him talking to another guest at the inn. Did you know he was moving his art gallery here to be close to me?" She sniffled, but no tears trickled down her cheeks, not even ghostly blue ones.

"Kevin told us about the move when he picked up Brutus," I said. There wasn't much else I could say to console her, so I didn't bother trying.

"The thought of him having to stay with those Abbott girls and not in his own home...well, it's just not right. Oh, and did I mention that Serena is the worst when it comes to money?"

"Really?" I asked, wondering what Evelyn had also overheard.

"Yes." Evelyn gripped the back of my seat and pulled herself closer. "She had the audacity to ask him if he knew who'd inherited my property. Then she wanted to know if it was him and if he'd be willing to sell it to her."

"Does Kevin inherit the property?" I asked.

"Of course, he does. I changed the will after Daniel died."

Evelyn's husband had been dead a while. If Kevin wanted to get rid of her to gain control of his inheritance, he would have done it long before now. "What did Kevin tell Serena about selling?" Jade had picked up enough of the conversation to ask.

"He knew I would never sell my home and told her absolutely not," Evelyn said with smug satisfaction as she slid back in her seat.

I smiled and shook my head to relay Evelyn's answer, then followed the car ahead of us into a graveled parking area that ran along the brick exterior wall surrounding the By the Bay Cemetery.

"It looks like the place is going to be busy tonight,"

Shawna said, twisting in her seat to stare out the window.

The sun had set less than an hour ago, and all the spots closest to the building housing the haunted house were already taken. Thankfully, Jade made an excellent co-pilot and found an empty spot within a reasonable walking distance.

Since a haunted tour was no place for purses, we locked all of ours in the trunk after stuffing bare essentials like money, keys, and lip gloss in our pockets. We were all dressed in jeans and jackets.

Jade was more into fashion than Shawna and me, so her pants and shirt leaned more toward designer casual. Since it took a while to get through the building and the urge to walk quickly after something jumped out and tried to grab us could happen anywhere, we had agreed that wearing comfortable shoes was best.

As soon as we got in line to purchase tickets, my thoughts drifted to the best way to help Evelyn. So far, the suspects on my list were dwindling, and finding new clues hadn't gone well. Evelyn was well-liked by everyone. I had yet to find anyone who held a grudge or had a reason to harm her.

From what I remembered of the crime scene, nothing had been torn apart. Other than her necklace, nothing else had been taken. I felt confident in ruling out a break-in. Her death seemed more personal, but without knowing the reason, it was difficult to figure out who wanted her dead.

The evening air had gotten colder. My friends and I stuffed our hands in our pockets and huddled closer to stay warm, which didn't do much good because of the overgrown insect standing next to us. Luckily, we weren't subjected to the increased drop in temperature very long.

"Since I don't have to pay to get in, I'm going inside to check things out," Evelyn snickered, then vanished.

"Our friendly spook disappeared again," I said, hoping she actually made it inside and didn't end up at the cemetery next door.

"Darn, I wanted her to see Nate's costume and makeup. I think he looks awesome," Shawna said.

"Oh yeah, what character is he playing this year?" Jade asked.

"He and the other spoofers are dressed like vampires, so avoid getting close to any coffins." Shawna hummed a spooky tune and formed claws with her fingers.

The spoofers was our nickname for the Supernatural Spoof Squashers, a group organized by Jade's brother Bryce. The club only had three members that I knew of, Myra Mitchell being the third. They were extremely knowledgeable about anything paranormal and had helped us research information in the past.

The volunteers had excellent costumes, and sometimes it took me a while to figure out who was playing which role. The settings inside seemed real, were exceptionally scary, and designed to elicit fear. You'd think knowing who was working in the haunted house ahead of time would minimize the scare factor, but no matter how many times I took the tour, my adrenaline kicked in, and I ended up screaming several times during the night.

"I take it your boyfriend will be the guy wrapping his cape around the cute girls and pretending to bite them in the neck," Jade said.

"I'd say that's a given," I chuckled.

"You two are not funny, and if you're trying to make me jealous, it's not working," Shawna harrumphed.

"Sure it isn't," Jade muttered, irritating Shawna even more.

The teasing ended when we moved up to pay. All the shop owners in town volunteered their time whenever there was an annual event. Besides spending a fun night out with my friends, I'd hoped to obtain information that might provide us with more clues. To keep the members of my family from offering their help, I'd made sure to pick a night I knew they'd all be working.

Grams and Mattie, dressed in similar Gypsy outfits

with colorful blue sashes and three-inch hooped earrings, had been tasked with collecting money. They were standing behind a table draped with a bright orange tablecloth and covered with Halloween images. Roles of tickets, a couple of hand stamps, and a cash box were the only things sitting on top of the table.

Roy was sitting behind them on a folding chair with its back propped against the building. "Ladies," he said, tipping his head in our general direction.

"Are you off duty tonight?" I asked since he was dressed in a pair of worn jeans and an old leather jacket instead of his sheriff's outfit.

"No, I'm working," Roy said. "You know how uptight the teenagers get when they see the uniform. I need to keep an eye on things, but I don't want to ruin their fun."

It seemed age had mellowed the sheriff, at least with some situations. I could remember several occasions when my friends and I were younger that Roy didn't have a problem ruining things for us. Or making sure our parents found out about them.

Other than a text to see if I was doing all right, I hadn't seen or spoken to Logan. "Is your nephew hanging around somewhere?" Roy knew Logan and I were dating, so I didn't feel uncomfortable asking the question.

"He was until we got a call about a break-in. He's over at the cemetery checking it out. I told him he might end up spending most of the night there."

Shimmying the wall and exploring the graveyard at night was a tradition for all the local teenagers, including those from neighboring towns. During the two weeks the haunted house was running, the town provided the graveyard with extra security because poor old Clyde Anderson, the evening caretaker, couldn't keep up.

Though none of them would admit it, a visit to the graveyard had probably been a thing when Roy, Grams, and Mattie were still in high school.

My teenage years were long past, but I hadn't outgrown

my dislike of tromping around headstones, even in the daylight hours. That hadn't seemed to matter not so long ago when Shawna insisted the three of us climb the wall and investigate Jessica's crime scene when we were trying to help find her killer.

They might be related, but I'd never witnessed Roy showing Logan any kind of favoritism since he'd relocated to town to work with him. Was sending his nephew to the cemetery his way of initiating him?

Elliott used to talk about the nights he worked in the cemetery around Halloween when he'd first gotten a job with the police force. Back then, I didn't believe in the paranormal and always thought parts of his stories were made up to impress my friends and me. Now I wondered if maybe he was telling the truth about everything he'd shared with us.

"Where's dad?" I asked Grams after handing her my money and taking a ticket.

"You know your father. He won't miss an opportunity to dress up and help Max scare the customers."

"What kind of costumes are they wearing this year?" Shawna held out her wrist to have it stamped with a cat standing on a pumpkin.

Kids weren't the only ones my dad and uncle enjoyed scaring. They'd frightened my friends and me enough times over the years for all of us to be wary and watch out for them. They also made a point of not letting us know which disguise they had collaborated on ahead of time.

"You know I've been sworn to secrecy and can't tell you," Grams chuckled.

Mattie pressed the stamp to Jade's wrist. "No one made me swear, so keep your eyes open for anything furry with fangs."

That helpful hint narrowed down the areas they could be working to one—the werewolf attraction. The upside to being a local and attending the haunted house every year was learning the layout. It didn't hurt that one or more family members usually volunteered to be on the committee. If a new attraction was added, we always knew ahead of time.

Shawna grinned. "Thanks, Mattie. I owe you big time."

"What about mom?" I held out my hand to be stamped. "Is she working inside as well?"

When it came to town-sponsored events, my mother made sure our family always participated. I was still trying to figure out a way to get out of taking her place on next year's Founders Day committee. Mostly because Serena was the one who ran it, which meant I had to put up with Lavender and her snide comments at every meeting.

"She's working the concession stand with Nadine," Grams said.

"I thought Nadine would be given out readings." Shawna's dejection wasn't a surprise. Nadine was our local fortuneteller, and my friend lived to have her palm read or hear about what the future had in store for her.

"She and Edith are taking turns. You'll have to stop by and ask her when she plans to take over again," Mattie said.

Edith had an uncanny ability of knowing things. Her predictions could be vague, and sometimes a little scary. I wasn't much for having my fortune read, but I would definitely go with Nadine if I had to choose between the two women.

"Guess you'll have to wait until later to find out if you and fang boy have a future together," Jade teased.

"I say we stop and see Edith. I'd be interested to hear what she has to say about you and Kevin." Shawna fluttered her eyelashes, then stuck her tongue out at Jade.

"We're, I'm..." Jade stammered and glared at Shawna.

I never understood why attending the town's events always brought out the terrible teens in my friends. Before their banter became an argument, I did what I did best, I stepped between them and hooked my arms through theirs. "Why don't we go inside?"

"You girls behave yourself and try not to find any more dead bodies," Roy said.

"We'll do our best... Not to find any, I mean." Jade giggled when Roy frowned.

I urged my friends toward the entrance and called over my shoulder, "See you guys later."

"I told you he thinks you're a murder magnet," Shawna stated proudly as soon as we were out of Roy's hearing range.

"I am not a murder magnet, and it's not my fault if I happen to be around whenever there's a dead body." It wasn't like I spent my spare time driving around town and waiting for someone to keel over. "Besides, if I remember correctly, you're the one who found Jake bobbing in the water."

"Okay, so I forgot about that. I guess that makes all of us murder magnets, then." Shawna grinned. "How awesome is that?"

"Oh yeah, that's totally spectacular," Jade said sarcastically.

"We need to keep an eye out for Elliott," I said once we were inside the dimly lit building. I could always count on him to inadvertently share clues.

"Why?" Shawna asked.

"I would imagine so she can find out what's going on in the case without Logan or Roy finding out about it," Jade said.

"Do either of you know where Elliott is working tonight?" Grams and Mattie would know, but asking them in front of Roy might have gotten me a lecture. I also couldn't risk him calling Elliott and warning him ahead of time.

"I'm not sure, but I could call and ask Nate." Shawna reached into her pocket to pull out her phone.

Elliott worked every night the haunted house was open, so I wasn't worried that he'd be here somewhere. "No, that's okay. We'll run into him eventually."

The place was set up to be one continuous maze, a winding path that moved the visitors from one setting to the next until they reached the exit on the opposite end of the building. The only exception was the fortune teller area and the concession stand. They were set up next to each other in an area separate from the tour.

For the cost of an additional ticket and waiting in an even longer line, anyone could hear about their future. Jade and I had spent more than one visit standing with Shawna after she'd convinced us that she absolutely had to have a reading. The upside to keeping her company was being able to snack while we waited.

"Besides, we wouldn't want you to interrupt Nate if he's in the middle of trying to bite someone." Jade dodged the smack she'd been expecting from Shawna, then laughed until we reached our first stop, which happened to be a witchy scenario.

There was eerie music playing in the background, and an orange fog similar to the stuff I'd seen at Evelyn's house covered the floor. Three witches in striking outfits moved around a cauldron chanting and cackling while they tossed things into the bubbling brew. It was difficult to determine who they were under all the makeup, but it didn't stop Jade from commenting that one of them could have been Lavender.

After that, we followed a path that led to a mock cemetery.

"Rylee, why didn't you tell us they added a new attraction?" Shawna gripped Jade's jacket sleeve as we inched our way between numerous headstones.

"Maybe because I didn't know anything about it," I said, then latched onto Jade's other sleeve.

It took a zombie uncle ambling toward us on my left for me to realize that my family forgetting to mention this particular display had been intentional. My assumption was reinforced when a zombie closely resembling my father moaned and ambled out of the shadows on the right, then reached for Shawna.

My brain knew the walking dead weren't real but forgot to communicate the message with the rest of my body. The impulse to run after releasing a wailing scream was squelched by my father's laughter. Max walked up next to him and gave him a congratulatory clap on the back.

"You two are not amusing," Jade said, even though she was chuckling with them. "Why are you dressed like zombies? We heard you were working in the werewolf attraction."

"Oh," Jade said when Max's smirk hinted that we'd been given wrong information on purpose.

"I can't believe Mattie lied to me," Shawna snapped indignantly. "I am banning her coffee shop for at least a week."

Jade and I shared a knowing look, then laughed even harder. We both knew Shawna wouldn't make it a day before wanting to stop and get her favorite latte.

My father walked over and stood next to me, then asked, "Is your invisible friend with you?"

I'd gotten a glimpse of glowing blue near a headstone in the corner right before I went into panic mode but hadn't realized it was Evelyn until my father asked.

"Rylee, please tell Max and Jonathan they were great," Evelyn managed to get out during a bout of laughter before she disappeared again.

I puffed out a sigh. "I'm afraid she left again, but she said to tell you the performance was great." My racing heart and my friend with blue streaked hair strongly disagreed.

After congratulating my uncle again, my father asked, "I don't suppose you can call her back and see if she'd like to move objects around for us? It would really add to the ambiance."

"Geez, dad, it's not like I have a special number to call the spirit world or anything."

"That's too bad," he said. "Maybe I should send the

spirit seeker back to Madame Minerva's and see if we can get you an upgrade."

"Dad," I said through gritted teeth.

He pulled me against his side. "I'm kidding."

Voices and footsteps echoed from the direction we'd traveled.

"It sounds like you're about to get some more unsuspecting victims," Jade said.

"Wonderful." Max clapped his hands, then headed back to his hiding spot with my father hurrying close behind him.

"Time to go," I said to Shawna and Jade, who didn't waste any time catching up with me.

The third set turned out to be Dr. Frankenstein's lab, complete with Elliott playing his hunchback assistant's role.

We stood off to the side and watched Elliott's performance, which was unexpectedly good. He'd convinced a sixteen-year-old girl to climb up on the table and pretend to be Frankenstein's monster while he pressed buttons and pulled levers to put on an electrical light show. Her friends, of which there were four, huddled nearby oohing and awwwing. Some of them even jumped when a loud boom accompanied a lightning bolt.

Once Elliott finished, the girls thanked him, then rushed to the next part of the tour. It wouldn't be long before my father and uncle finished terrorizing the group who'd been following us, so I needed to hurry if I wanted to get any clues. I leaned towards Shawna and Jade. "You guys go ahead. I'll catch up in a few minutes."

Since we'd already discussed my reason for wanting to talk to Elliott, they left without asking.

I knew from experience that compliments usually worked to get him talking. "Hey, Elliott, I really like the costume. It's even better than last year's."

"Thanks." He pressed several buttons on a panel, and the overhead lights dimmed. "I did the makeup with a kit I bought at your family's shop."

"I'd say you did an excellent job." Squeals in the distance prompted me to forego any more niceties. "I know you're not supposed to share anything about the cases you're working on, but Grams and Evelyn were close. I know it would mean a lot to her if you could tell me how Evelyn died or if you're any closer to finding the killer."

Elliott was also one of Grams's tarot reading customers. When it looked as if he wasn't going to share any information, I said, "Maybe she'll even give you a discount on your next reading." I'd been careful to insinuate that it was a possibility, so I couldn't be accused of bribery.

Elliott tucked his hands in his lab coat pockets. "I can't tell you the names of our suspects, but I can tell you this is one of the strangest cases I've ever worked on."

During my short stint as a novice sleuther, I'd discovered the best way to get people to open up and obtain information was by acting agreeably. "Really?" Elliott was much easier than most. All he needed was a little enthusiasm to continue, so I didn't press him any further.

"Yep." He gazed right, then left. "We found some dirt tracks on the carpet in the hallway near the top of the staircase. The weird thing is the prints stopped in the middle of the floor, and not near any doorways."

"That is odd," I said, placing a hand on my chest. "You don't think you're dealing with something supernatural, do you?" I may have recently been introduced to the paranormal world, but after talking to Evelyn, I was fairly certain a flesh and blood person was responsible for her death.

"You never know. That house is pretty old. Who's to say it isn't haunted?"

It was haunted all right, but not in the way Elliott was thinking.

CHAPTER TEN

"Did you enjoy your surprise?" my mother asked after placing a large plastic basket filled with French fries, along with some paper plates and a handful of ketchup packets on the table Shawna, Jade, and I had gathered around in the haunted house concession area. Her hair was secured loosely at her nape and the medieval costume she was wearing made her look as if she belonged in a renaissance fair.

I knew she was referring to the scare we'd gotten from my father and uncle. Personally, I'd be quite content not to receive any more surprises for the rest of the year, maybe the next five years as well.

"Yeah, sure." Shawna made an annoyed face. "I look forward to being terrorized by Jonathan and Max every year."

"Be glad it's only once a year," my mother said. "It would be more often if those two thought they could get away with it."

I didn't know why my mother thought my father's antics were limited to Halloween. It was only a few months ago that he'd caused me to have what I considered a near-death experience when he sent me the spirit seeker.

"No doubt." Jade grabbed a fry.

After noticing that more people were arriving, my mother said, "I need to get back and help Nadine. You girls have fun with the rest of the tour, and I'll see you in the morning."

I waited until she'd slipped behind the counter to take an order from the next person in line before speaking. "I think we should check out that upstairs hallway tonight while Evelyn's house is empty." I'd already filled Shawna and Jade in on what I considered a new clue from Elliott and didn't need to provide an additional explanation. I hated asking them to cut our visit short, but after talking to Elliott, all I could think about was the mysterious dirty footprints the police had discovered. I was curious to find out how they'd gotten there.

The day I found Evelyn, I didn't go upstairs, and I hadn't seen the prints for myself. If Vivian had cleaned that morning, wouldn't she have noticed the dirt on the carpet and said something to Evelyn? Since she hadn't, it could only mean the prints belonged to the killer and were left behind after Vivian had gone for the day.

"You mean while the police are preoccupied, and our chances of not being caught are better, don't you?" Jade finished taking a sip of her soda and set it back on the table.

"Pretty much," I said.

"I'm not saying we shouldn't do it, but Evelyn's house is still a crime scene. Don't you think we should get Kevin's permission to go inside first?" Jade asked.

"Are you sure it's his permission you're after? Or is it because you want to see him again?" Shawna squeezed a packet of ketchup on her paper plate.

Jade's cheeks flushed. "If I admit that I like him, will you stop pestering me?"

"Nooo," Shawna and I both said at the same time.

"If you're worried about the criminal aspect of things, you guys can always wait outside while I check it out," I said once Jade stopped grumbling about getting new friends.

"We aren't letting you go in there alone." Shawna narrowed her eyes at Jade. "Are we?"

"Of course not," Jade huffed. "Why would you think such a thing?"

"Good," I said triumphantly. "If Evelyn's house is still taped off, there's a good chance the prints haven't been removed yet. We might even be able to figure out how they got there in the first place."

"Don't you think the police, who are trained for this kind of thing, would have already figured it out?" Shawna asked.

"Not according to Elliott. He said this is the strangest case he's ever worked."

"So, what makes you think we'll be able to solve the mystery when they can't," Jade asked.

"Because we have something they don't have." I grinned.

"Oh yeah, and what is that?" Shawna asked.

"Someone who knows the house and can walk through walls." I hadn't actually seen Evelyn move through any inanimate objects yet, but I knew it was possible. Success relied heavily on whether or not she made an appearance during our search. Now that my friends had agreed to help, I decided to keep that particular detail to myself.

"Hey, wait a minute," Shawna said. "If we leave now, you won't be able to see Nate's costume."

"I'm pretty sure he'll understand if he knows we're doing this to help Evelyn," I said.

"Consider it a covert mission," Jade added. "One that you can't tell anyone about, not even a boyfriend."

To keep Shawna from disagreeing, I said, "At least not until we're done investigating."

Shawna grabbed a couple of French fries from the basket, then dipped them in the red splotch on her plate. "I guess I could tell him we had to leave because Jade wasn't feeling well."

"Or," Jade said. "You could tell him *you* feel sick."

"That would be dishonest." Shawna shoved the fries in her mouth after shooting Jade a disgusted glare.

"And telling Nate I'm sick, when I'm really not, is being truthful?" Jade asked.

"It doesn't count because you're not his girlfriend."

Frustration flickered in Jade's blue eyes. "That makes perfect sense. Thanks for explaining it to me."

Most of the time, Shawna's logic evaded Jade and me, but we'd learned from experience not to argue with her about it.

Content that her idea had been accepted, Shawna retrieved the cell phone from her back pocket and keyed in a text. A few seconds later, she received a response from Nate. "Awww, how sweet." She glanced up after reading his message. "He said to tell you he hopes you feel better and included a sad face emoji."

When the cell buzzed again, Jade leaned closer to see the screen. "What else did he say?"

"Do you mind?" Shawna yanked the screen from Jade's view. "This one's personal." Once Shawna had finished oohing at whatever Nate had said, she slipped the cell back into her pocket, switching her attention to me. "So, mission leader, how do you plan on sneaking out of here without being seen? We can't use the emergency door because it will trigger an alarm."

"I believe I can help with that." I was proud that I'd barely twitched, and the fries I'd been holding hadn't gone flying when Evelyn appeared in the empty chair next to me. Even more so after getting a glimpse of the shimmering blue ninja outfit she was wearing. On a woman her age, it seemed a little daunting. But if she could help us get out of here, I'd worry about any potential nightmares the image was going to cause later.

***

As promised, Evelyn showed us how to find the corridor running behind the exhibits that took us to a side door and eventually out into the parking lot. All the volunteers were too busy working the main attractions to notice us.

Once we reached the entrance to Evelyn's driveway, I pulled my car off the road, then glanced in the rearview mirror. "Evelyn, is there somewhere I can park where we won't be seen?"

I wasn't inclined to participate in criminal activities, but now that I could see ghosts, they seemed to happen frequently. Getting caught was not part of the plan. I justified the guilt I was feeling by telling myself that I had Evelyn's permission to go inside the house.

The odds of running into Kevin were slim since he was staying at the Beaumont. I hadn't heard whether or not the police considered Gary's cottage part of their crime scene. If they hadn't, and he was home, I didn't want him to see or hear my vehicle. And if we needed to make a quick getaway, I reasoned that it would be better to approach the house on foot.

"There's a narrow drive up here on the left that leads to the back of the property. It's not in very good condition, and I think Gary is the only one who ever uses it to haul things around in his truck," Evelyn said.

"How far is it from the house?" I asked.

"It's a little bit of a walk, but not too bad."

Discovering there was another way to access the property provided a way for Evelyn's attacker to reach the house without being seen. If the intruder had used the front door to make a hasty exit the day Grams and I had arrived, it would explain why we hadn't seen them. Finding out about the road's existence, coupled with Gary knowing about it, increased his chances of being the person my friends and I were searching for.

"Evelyn says there's a place up ahead where we can park, but we'll have to walk to reach the house," I said to Jade and Shawna. After getting back on the two-lane road and driving a little farther, I found the junction she'd specified. The dirt road was rutted and worn. It wound its way through the trees and was only wide enough for one vehicle. I would have preferred to drive without my headlights, but it was too dark to see where I was going.

It didn't appear as if there were any places to turn around. I didn't want to drive the entire length of the road and find out it ended up near the cottage. Backing out the same way I came seemed like the best option, so I didn't drive far before parking my car.

"This isn't spooky at all," Shawna said once we were all standing outside.

"Says the person who has no problem tromping through graveyards," I said sarcastically and shot her a disbelieving glance. Usually, I was the one who didn't like traipsing through dark places in the middle of the night.

"Hey, at least the cemetery had lighted pathways and overhead lights on the mausoleums," Shawna said as she buttoned her jacket. "Who knows what might be hiding out here?"

My courage was doing fine until she reminded me that things could be stalking us from the shadows.

"You mean like spiders and rats?" Jade's comment had Shawna immediately checking the ground and scooting away from my car as if something was now hiding underneath. I'd forgotten that she wasn't fond of rodents or eight-legged insects, specifically those who could weave webs.

I opened the trunk and pulled out my backpack, which hadn't been removed since we'd been on a similar adventure. After handing everyone a flashlight, I hooked the bag's strap on my shoulder. "Evelyn, which way do we go?" I had an idea which way we needed to head but preferred some guidance in case my sense of direction was wrong.

"It's been a while since I've been out here, but I'm pretty sure it's this way." Evelyn headed through a gap in the trees, her shimmering blue body easy to see in the blanket of darkness surrounding us. I flipped on my light and followed after her. A few seconds later, two more beams joined mine, bouncing off the ground and nearby trees as Shawna and Jade trailed behind me.

It took us about five minutes to reach the edge of the woods and the lawn running along the side of the house. The sky was overcast, and the surrounding area was dark. The tall trees blocked out any light the moon and stars might have provided. Even with our flashlights, everything was cast in shadows, and seeing where we were going had been difficult.

"Now that we're here, how do you plan to get inside?" Jade stopped next to me and stared at the house. "It's not like Evelyn has a key, or any of us is equipped with a set of lock picks."

"I know where we can find a key," Evelyn said, then started moving toward the front of the house.

I wanted to scold her about leaving a key outside. It was the easiest way for a thief, or killer in her case, to access her home. I was afraid if I did say something, she'd get upset and disappear before telling me where the key was hidden.

"Evelyn knows where to find a key," I said to my friends as they trudged after me.

"Is that the cottage?" Jade stopped halfway across the lawn and flashed her light in the direction of the building I'd seen the day I'd been searching for Brutus.

"Yes," Evelyn and I said at the same time.

"It doesn't look like anyone is home," Shawna said.

"Or Gary is already sleeping," I said. The exterior light above the door was on, but all the windows were dark. "Maybe we should keep moving." Doing it as quietly as possible wouldn't be a bad idea either.

If Gary was home, we didn't need him to come outside and find us. I didn't want to consider what might happen if he was the one who'd pushed Evelyn down the stairs. My friends must have been thinking the same thing. They didn't need any encouragement to put some distance between us and the cottage.

Evelyn passed the front porch, then stopped next to a tree behind the life-size ghost I'd seen the last time I was here. Its dilapidated form was lying on the ground because its air supply had been terminated.

"I hid the key in there," Evelyn said.

"Where?" I asked, expecting to find some plant pots or rocks sitting on the ground.

"In the bottom of the middle birdhouse."

I swept my flashlight in the direction she was pointing and saw three hand-crafted houses mounted on separate wooden poles. Each one was painted a different color and trimmed in white. They reminded me of miniature mansions designed for birds.

"There's a secret compartment underneath," Evelyn said with a grin.

I walked over to the middle pole. "Evelyn said the key is hidden in the bottom of the birdhouse." While I searched for the key, Jade kept her flashlight aimed at the wooden structure. After pushing, pulling, and prodding every inch of wood along the bottom without finding the hiding place, I finally gave up. "Okay, Evelyn, how do you get it open?"

Evelyn smirked. "Sorry, you need to push the end of the perch into the house."

As soon as I did what she'd said, a small drawer containing a key popped out of the miniature porch. I took the key and pushed the drawer back into its hiding place, glad I'd squelched the urge to scold her about it earlier.

"That's rather ingenious." Shawna moved closer, running her beam along the edges to inspect the craftsmanship.

"Daniel built it," Evelyn said. "He loved tinkering with puzzle boxes and such. We have them all over the house."

After repeating what Evelyn said, I asked, "Did anyone else know your key was in there?" Was there possibly another suspect I'd overlooked?

"No, Kevin has his own key to the house in case of emergencies, and so does Gary. I'm usually here when Vivian comes to clean. And if I'm not, then Gary lets her in."

"So Gary and Kevin were the only other people besides you that had access?" I reiterated.

Evelyn nodded, then squinted. "I know what you're thinking." The ghostly wrinkles around her eyes deepened the more irritated she became. "There's no way either of them would do this to me."

"I believe you." Or at least I agreed with her believing that neither of them was guilty. Kevin had a strong alibi, but I hadn't had a chance to talk to Gary yet, so he was still on my list. As soon as Evelyn appeared calm, I moved the conversation onto what I hoped was a safer topic. "Maybe we should go inside and check out those footprints."

"I like that plan." Jade glanced toward the end of the house closest to the cottage. "The sooner we can get out of here, the better."

I ignored the gruesome knocker, which both my friends thought was terrific, and stepped aside so they could enter ahead of me. Shawna didn't comment on the creepy noise the front door made when I opened and closed it. She did, however, squeak when her light beam landed on the spider in the middle of a fake web covering a corner of the foyer. She spun around, the beam from her flashlight landing on my face. "You could've mentioned that thing was hanging there before we came inside."

"It wasn't exactly on the top of my covert sleuthing list," I said, walking past the cauldron and using my own beam to find the bottom of the stairs.

We couldn't use the inside lights, not without the risk of Gary or someone from the inn seeing them. "Evelyn, before we investigate the footprints, why don't you go through exactly what happened." I grabbed the railing and slowly worked my way up the stairs with my friends following closely behind me. The moon and stars viewed through the second-floor windows provided more light and made seeing a little better.

"Where were you standing when the intruder attacked you?" I asked Evelyn.

"Right about here." Evelyn stopped on the landing a foot away from the first step. I pointed so my friends would know what she'd said.

"It's a miracle Daniel didn't end up all over the place," Shawna said after studying the stairs.

"Shawna," Jade snapped.

"What? I was complementing Evelyn's excellent grip."

"Thank you," Evelyn said. "It was a pretty spectacular feat if I don't mind saying so myself."

"Evelyn says thanks. Now can we…" The front door creaking as it opened, followed by a loud thump when it shut, had all three of us screaming in unison as if we'd spent months practicing the high-pitches together. If Evelyn had chimed in, I didn't hear her because she'd been too startled to stick around.

"Rylee, is that you?" Grams's voice echoed up the staircase along with the appearance of three separate beams of light.

She didn't sound surprised to find me in the house. I wondered why my grandmother was here and not at the haunted house where I'd left her.

"Pay up." Grams held out her hand to Mattie when they'd reached the top of the stairs. "I told you they'd be here."

"Grams, what are *you* doing here?" I asked.

"After Elliott told me about the footprints, I called

Gary and asked him if he'd let us in so we could investigate," Grams said. "It's incredible the amount of information offering a discount on a reading will get you."

I should have known she'd try to question Elliott when she couldn't coerce anything out of Roy. "And you didn't think to share that little tidbit before Max and Jonathan scared the pooper scoopers out of us?" Shawna asked.

"Halloween only comes once a year, and I wasn't about to ruin their fun," Grams said.

I scowled. "But it's okay if your only granddaughter and her friends end up traumatized for life."

Grams flicked her wrist and tsked. "You three have been terrorized plenty, and you look like you're doing fine to me."

Mattie started laughing. Even Gary, who I'd bet rarely smiled, had formed a semi-grin. It wasn't long before Shawna, Jade, and I joined in.

When the laughter finally died down, I said to Grams, "Now that you've confirmed none of us need therapy, maybe we should get back to investigating."

"I agree," Grams said. "The haunted house should have shut down by now. With all the teenagers running around town playing pranks, Roy might decide to stop by or send Logan to check and make sure they didn't mess with his crime scene."

As much as I wanted to see Logan, the idea of being caught inside the house by him sent pulses of anxiety rippling through my system.

Shawna held out her arms before any of us could take a step. "Be careful. We don't want to mess up the evidence."

"What evidence?" Jade swept her light across the carpet. "There aren't any footprints. It looks like someone had dirt on the bottom of their shoes and left little clumps on the carpet."

"That's disappointing," Mattie said, aiming her light in the same direction.

"I should have known Elliott was exaggerating,"

Grams said. "That boy always did have a knack for being dramatic."

So did my grandmother, but I wasn't about to say it out loud.

"At least he got the part about them disappearing right," I said, flashing my light on the carpet where they ended near the wall.

"Gary, do you have any idea how the dirt got in here?" Even though I considered him a suspect, I tried my best not to sound like I was accusing him of anything.

Gary shrugged. "I had no idea it was here until Grams told me." After glimpsing the dirt, he walked over to a landscape picture mounted on the wall. "But if what I suspect is right, then I know how someone else might have tracked the dirt in here."

"You do?" I asked.

"Pretty sure." Gary ran his fingers along the frame. After hearing a click, a gap appeared in the wooden panel. "What I don't know is who else knew it was here and how to open it."

Shawna pulled the panel wider, then aimed her light inside. "It's a secret passageway. How cool is that?"

"Not very cool if something decides to jump out at you," Jade said, hovering next to her.

"Where does it go?" I asked Gary as I leaned closer to get a glimpse of a spiraling staircase instead of the spooky corridor I'd expected.

"It goes down to the first floor and a door on the backside of the house," Gary said. "There's another button on the frame that will open it from here, but it can also be opened from outside if you know how to find the latch."

"I didn't see any door when I was looking for Brutus, did you?" I asked Grams.

"Only the ones by the patio," she said.

Gary stepped away from the wall. "That's because it's hidden behind a wall of bushes."

"Did Evelyn know this was here?" Grams asked Gary.

Shawna and Jade gave me inquiring looks. They must have assumed Evelyn was listening and were waiting for me to share her answer. I mouthed the word "gone" so they'd know she had vanished again.

"I honestly don't know." Gary scratched the graying stubble on his chin. "I'd forgotten all about it until now. I can't imagine Evelyn or her sisters even knew about it. The staircase is pretty old. Their father didn't want them playing inside or using it to sneak outside. He hung the picture to hide the inside mechanisms and planted the bushes when they were pretty young."

"Well, somebody figured out it was here and decided to open it up again." Grams placed a hand on my arm. "It would also explain why we didn't see anyone leaving through the front door when we arrived the other day. And why Brutus was digging when we found him."

"It's too bad Brutus can't talk," I said.

"Why is that?" Mattie asked.

If the steps were old, they were most likely the source of the creaking Evelyn had heard. Testing a theory about the door slamming noise I'd heard the day Grams and I had found her body, I motioned for everyone to step back, then gave the panel a push. Sure enough, when it realigned with the wall, the secret door made a noticeable thump followed by a click when the lock snapped back into place.

"Because there's a good chance Brutus saw Evelyn's killer."

CHAPTER ELEVEN

Occasionally, like today, Jade and Shawna ended up having the same Friday off. Now that my parents were back, my schedule was a little more flexible, so after the long night we'd had, I decided to take the morning off and spend time with them. Instead of meeting at their apartment, they decided to stop by mine. The clue I'd gotten from Elliott had led us to the secret staircase, but it hadn't provided us with any new suspects.

After a lengthy and depressing conversation recapping what we'd learned so far, which wasn't helpful, we did what we always did to make ourselves feel better. We walked across the street to Mattie's place.

Jade and I were determined to wipe away our melancholy by indulging in a spectacular chocolate dessert, so neither of us reminded Shawna about her plan to ban the shop.

The early morning crowd had come and gone. The place was still busy but not packed, and we were able to snag a corner table near the front window. Once we'd ordered, paid for our desserts and drinks, and settled into our seats, my thoughts drifted to Evelyn. I hadn't spoken to her since our less than successful covert mission the night before. She was either experiencing a bout of depression like my friends and me, or she hadn't been able to home in on my location yet.

"I'm out of ideas," I said, hating the feeling of frustration that came with not being able to solve Evelyn's murder. It hadn't helped that I hadn't spoken to Logan in a couple of days. Even if discussing my ability hadn't caused some tension between us, asking him for help crossed an unspoken relationship line I wasn't willing to break.

Grams didn't have the same kind of conflict with Roy, and even if she did, she still would have tried to get information out of him. It didn't make me happy to hear that she and Mattie hadn't gotten anywhere either. Roy seemed happy to spend time with them at the haunted house, but I'd been certain he was aware of their intentions and had avoided answering any questions about the case.

"Me too," Jade said, blowing on her coffee, then taking a sip.

"I still think Gary is a possibility. For all we know, he could've shown us that secret panel to keep suspicion off himself," Shawna said, her eyes never leaving the page of the newspaper she'd brought along with us. Evelyn's death had made headline news for several days, and Shawna was perusing one of the articles, this one focused on Kevin being her only heir. It wouldn't be long until she flipped further back to find the horoscope section. The section I dreaded.

"I don't think he was faking his emotions," I said. "He seemed sincere about helping us find Evelyn's killer." I took a bite of my brownie oozing with hot fudge and caramel, then let the chocolate-infused deliciousness slowly glide over my tongue before chewing and swallowing.

"Don't forget he has an alibi. He was helping Max set up the pumpkin patch." I swirled my fork through the air. "There's only one main road near Evelyn's house. If he'd sneaked away early, I would have passed him on my way there."

"Even so, he lives on the property and has keys to the house," Jade said. "Why go through all the trouble of using that old staircase?"

"Maybe he was after her valuables and planned to steal them a little at a time," Shawna said.

"Evelyn does have quite a few antiques sitting around," I said. "But if Gary was after any of them, he's had plenty of opportunities to take whatever he wanted without having to push her down the stairs."

Jade placed her napkin on her lap. "And why take the necklace and nothing else? Other than sentimental value, it wasn't worth anything, was it?"

"Not that I'm aware of." At least that's what I'd assumed, which made trying to figure out who the killer was so frustrating. I stared outside, more focused on Jade's questions than the pedestrians walking by. The necklace had come up in several of my talks with Evelyn, but I couldn't recall her ever telling me why someone would want it.

"I'm still not convinced. Maybe we need to ask Evelyn what she thinks." Shawna rubbed her arms, then gave me a quick glance. "She hasn't shown up yet, has she?"

No one had opened a door, but the area around our table had suddenly chilled. I scanned the room, and sure enough, Evelyn had appeared near the dessert display case. She'd gone back to wearing her witch's costume, but her hair was bright pink, and it looked as if it had been sprinkled with glitter. She heaved a heavy sigh at the delectables, then came to hover next to our table.

Trying to appear nonchalant, I scooted out the extra chair so she could take a seat.

"Tell Shawna that Gary has worked for my family for years. If he wanted to get rid of me, which I don't believe for a second that he did, he could have put poison in my tea to make it look like I died naturally." Evelyn tapped the table. "Or he could have pushed me off the bluff behind the house and told everyone I fell."

"I'll tell her," I said, then kept my voice low and repeated what Evelyn had said to my friends.

Shawna leaned forward and spoke toward the empty seat. "Geez, you've really given some thought to the whole demise thing, haven't you?"

"I seem to have quite a bit of time on my hands," Evelyn said. "Not to mention, I'd really like to find out who did this so I can move on and see my sweet Daniel again."

"She has, and she's convinced it's not Gary," I said.

"Fine." Shawna slumped her shoulders and went back to reading the newspaper.

"It sounds like we've reached a dead end." Jade absently picked at her slice of raspberry swirl cheesecake. "Besides, with no more clues or suspects, where does that leave us?"

"You could always ask Ev...I mean our friend what is so important about her necklace and why she thinks someone would want to, you know..." Shawna grabbed her own throat and made a choking noise.

"That's easy, it's..." Evelyn's response was cut off by the sound of a tinkling bell.

Most of the businesses along Swashbuckler Blvd. had bells attached to the frame above their doors to announce customers, Mattie's place included. When we heard the melodic noise, my friends and I reacted automatically by looking up to see who had arrived.

It was Molly Jacobs. She worked for Lavender and Serena at the Beaumont Inn. Her main job was operating the registration desk, but she occasionally helped out with other guest-related tasks. Personally, I thought she deserved an award, maybe even a raise, for regularly having to deal with the annoying sisters.

"Hey, guys," Molly said, giving us a wave before walking over to our table. "How's it going?"

Her dark hair was pulled away from her face with

combs on both sides of her head. Judging by the black pumps and navy blue skirt not covered by her thigh-length jacket, I assumed she was either on her way or had recently left somewhere important.

Shawna placed her finger on the page to track where she'd been reading, then looked up and smiled. "Hey, Molls, how are things out at the inn?"

Molly shrugged. "Busy. Almost all the rooms are booked with tourists who came here to visit the haunted house."

"Are you off today?" Jade was into fashion and would have noted Molly's attire and asked out of curiosity or to be polite.

"No, I stopped to get some coffee on my way to work." Molly glanced around the room to see if anyone was listening. "You didn't hear it from me, but the brands Lavender stocks for the employees aren't very good."

"I promise not to say a word." I was pretty sure that after our run-in at the pumpkin patch, I was the last person Lavender would want to converse with or take coffee brand selection advice from.

Molly's gaze wandered to the newspaper, the bold headline about Evelyn's death hard to miss. "Such a shame about Evelyn. I heard you and Grams were the ones to"— she paused to swallow—"find her."

Yeah had become my conditioned response for the past two days. I didn't want to discuss Evelyn's death, not with her sitting next to me and looking as if she might start sobbing.

"I really liked Evelyn," Molly said, releasing a long, drawn-out sigh. "She could be a little eccentric at times, but she was such a sweet person and hosted the best parties."

I'd expected Evelyn to disagree with the first part of Molly's statement. Instead, she straightened in her seat and grinned.

"I totally agree," Shawna said.

"Me too," Jade added.

I was proud of Evelyn for not already poofing out. Not that I could share my thoughts about it with Molly. "I still can't believe Evelyn's gone," I said, drawing a snort from her ghost.

Gossiping was a favorite pass-time in Cumberpatch, a skill honed to perfection by many of its residents. I didn't really believe Molly would know anything important that could help us, but it didn't hurt to ask. "Do you have any idea who'd purposely want to take her life?"

Molly pursed her lips and crossed her arms. "Her sister Lydia comes to mind. Personality-wise, those two are *completely* different."

"How so?" I pretended that I didn't already know Lydia was a pushy, self-centered individual and the complete opposite of Evelyn.

"The woman is insufferable. I can't tell you how many times she's called the front desk to complain in the last couple of days. I'll be glad when she leaves."

"Is her husband Harold as bad as she is?" Shawna asked.

I didn't think so since he'd seemed somewhat timid when I'd seen him at Evelyn's.

"Oh, no. He's been here for over a week and usually keeps to himself," Molly said.

Shocked, I dropped my fork, then fumbled to catch it before it fell to the floor. "What do you mean he's been here for over a week? I thought he and Lydia just got to town, that they'd traveled together." Though after thinking about it, Lydia had told Logan *she'd* arrived, not *they'd* arrived.

"He does quite a bit of traveling for his business," Molly said. "They arrived separately."

"I had no idea he was here," Evelyn said right afterward.

Surely, since they were related, I would've thought he'd give Evelyn a call whenever he was in town. "Does he stay at the inn a lot?" The question was directed at both of them.

"Yes, once sometimes twice a month." Molly looked up as if in thought. "I don't ever remember him staying for more than a couple of days before. Maybe his business lasted longer than he expected, or maybe he decided to stick around for Evelyn's party." She pushed up the sleeve of her jacket to glance at her watch. "Anyway, it was great seeing you guys, but I better get going; otherwise, I'll have to listen to Lavender's complaints for the rest of the day."

"We definitely wouldn't want that," I said.

"See you later." Molly spun around and headed for the counter to place her order.

I was anxious to discuss what we'd learned from Molly but decided to wait until she'd left the shop. My friends must have had similar thoughts. Jade hurried to finish her dessert. Shawna flipped the newspaper to the section I dreaded, then quickly scanned the daily horoscopes, no doubt checking to see how the rest of our day was going to be impacted. With any luck, she'd keep the future prophecies to herself.

I sipped my coffee, keeping a periphery eye on Molly's progression while contemplating our newest clue. As soon as the door closed behind her, I shifted to give Evelyn my full attention. "Okay, now tell me... What is so special about that necklace?"

CHAPTER TWELVE

After running into Molly at Mattie's place, the discussion Shawna, Jade, and I'd been having with Evelyn had reached a confidential and shouldn't be discussed in front of others level, so we'd gone back to my apartment to finish it. For some reason, which I attributed to burning brain cells, solving crimes tended to cause rumbling stomachs in all three of us.

We were also certain, at least mostly, that Harold was the one who'd pushed Evelyn down the stairs. So, after consuming some ham and cheese sandwiches along with a large bag of chips, we'd crafted a plan to prove it. A plan that included a visit to the police station.

Shawna and Jade had no problem helping me strategize, but they'd decided it would be best if I went alone when it came to meeting with the sheriff. Since Grams was good at coercing Roy, at least most of the time, I'd thought about asking her to go along for support. An idea I quickly dismissed after considering all the ways she could make things worse.

Finessing Roy into returning Daniel's urn and releasing the crime scene would go a lot easier if my grandmother didn't accidentally—more likely intentionally—tell him we needed both things to catch Evelyn's killer.

Initially, Shawna and Jade thought I should ask Logan, but given the uncertain way we'd left things, and his penchant for advising me not to get involved in his cases, I wasn't sure he'd agree to help.

Since I didn't want to leave Barley at home alone for the afternoon, Shawna had dressed him up in the costume she'd gotten him and dropped him off at the shop.

Now that I was parked in the lot outside the Cumberpatch police department, deciding to go inside and follow through with our plan was a debate I seemed to be losing. I continued to grip the steering wheel and stare at the brick building until Evelyn drew me from my thoughts. "Is there a reason you're not going inside?"

I'd been so busy formulating what I was going to say to Roy that I'd forgotten she'd agreed to accompany me in case he asked me questions that only she could answer.

"No, I guess not." I reluctantly opened the door and scooted out of the car.

This was the first time Evelyn and I were in public without my friends or family's additional presence to act as buffers for our conversations. Pretending I was on the phone was the best way to talk to her without attracting unwanted attention from others. Not that I wasn't already being noticed because of the witchy rumors Lavender had taken great pleasure in spreading.

Since I couldn't keep my cell pressed to my ear the entire time we were inside, Evelyn had agreed to only talk when necessary. Once we entered the building, I gave Evelyn a reassuring smile, then walked up to the counter stretched along the back half of the reception area.

There was an officer with dark hair sitting on the other side of the counter. His head was down, and he was concentrating on some papers in an open file. "Excuse me," I said.

He jerked his head up, his irritated frown gradually transforming into a forced smile. "Can I help you?" He smoothed the front of his uniform as he got to his feet.

I'd never met him before, but his face seemed familiar, though I couldn't decide from where. "Yes." I swallowed. "I'd like to see sheriff Dixon please."

"Do you have an appointment?" he asked.

"No, I…"

"Rylee." Logan appeared in the doorway leading to another part of the building. He sounded surprised to see me.

Evelyn, who'd been determined only minutes ago to help me, gasped and faded. "Great," I muttered before realizing both men had heard me. Not only was I ghost less, but Logan probably thought my remark had been directed at him.

"What are you doing here?" Logan walked into the room and dropped the folder he was carrying into a wire basket on the end of the counter.

I thought it was promising that he hadn't made an excuse to duck back the way he came and avoid me altogether.

"She came to see Roy," the officer, who only seconds ago acted as if I was bothering him, was quick to answer.

I stifled a groan and narrowed my eyes at the overly helpful male, imaging what I'd like to say to him if Logan hadn't been in the room and there wasn't a desk between us.

"Oh." Logan masked the disappointment on his face but hadn't managed to keep it out of his voice. "I'll see that she gets there." He placed his hand on the small of my back and urged me toward the hallway on the left.

The last time I'd been here, we'd taken the same corridor, and I knew it passed Roy's office and eventually ended near the interrogation area. Having been a suspect in Jessica's murder, I was well acquainted with one of those rooms.

Instead of taking me to my expected destination, he led me down another hallway and into an office I'd never seen before. The average-sized room was furnished with a desk, two visitor chairs, and a tall metal filing cabinet stuffed in a corner. "Is this your office?" I asked since I hadn't visited him at work since he'd moved to Cumberpatch.

"Uh-huh." He paused in the doorway, then as an afterthought, asked, "Can I get you something to drink? The coffee's not the greatest, but we have a soda machine or bottled water."

"No, I'm good." I would have taken him up on his offer, but I didn't think any liquid sustenance would help the flutters in my stomach.

He closed the door behind him. "I hope you don't mind, but I wanted to talk to you first before taking you to see Roy." He motioned for me to sit in one of the chairs in front of his desk.

"Not at all." I relaxed a little when he took the seat next to me and not the one adjacent to his computer.

"I'm sorry I haven't called," he said.

Besides being consumed with finding Evelyn's killer, I'd spent the last two days stressing about whether or not Logan would ever want to see me again. Remaining rational didn't always work when I was emotionally invested in something. I focused on how hard it was for me to accept my new abilities and tried to be understanding when he didn't call.

"It's okay. I figured you were busy with work and trying to find Evelyn's killer." I should have been angry and not make excuses for him. Truthfully, I was still feeling a little guilty for not telling him about my ghost-seeing ability in the first place.

"I was, I am, but that's no reason to let so much time go by without reaching out to you." He swept his hand through his hair. "I'd planned to see you at the haunted house after I ran into your father, and he told me you and your friends would be there later. Unfortunately, some teenagers decided to place a fake corpse near a headstone in the cemetery. They nearly gave Clyde a heart attack, or so he said. I got the impression he's seen a lot over the years and doesn't scare easily."

Hearing he'd wanted to see me had my pulse racing. It would have been nice if my dad had mentioned he'd spoken to Logan, though I didn't think it would have kept me from stressing about our situation. "So, what did you want to talk about?" I figured if I asked first, I might not have to explain why I was here to see Roy and not him.

"I want to apologize if I sounded abrupt the last time we'd talked, and was hoping we could finish our discussion about your ghost thing." He reassured me that the talk wasn't going to be entirely serious when he grinned. "Is that the correct terminology?"

I smiled back. "I honestly don't know, but it works for me."

He pulled my hand into his lap. "I want you to know that I do believe unexplained phenomena does exist, but my job deals in facts and is governed by my logical side."

"And what is your logical side telling you now?" I asked, bombarded by a new wave of flutters.

"That even though you have a slightly"—he paused as if searching for the right word—"unique family, I know you're an intelligent woman and wouldn't fabricate something like being able to see spirits."

"So you're saying you like my eccentric family, you believe that I can talk to ghosts, and you think I'm smart?"

"Yes, to all of those things," Logan said, inching closer.

I thought for sure I'd be enjoying a makeup kiss until the temperature in the room dropped enough for Logan to notice and pull away from me. "Do you feel a chill?"

"Bad time?" Evelyn stood in the corner smirking and shimmering in a biker's costume complete with a leather jacket and riding boots. Seeing her lastest outfit made me shudder, and I tried not to imagine what she'd look like straddling a motorcycle.

I fought the urge to respond with a sarcastic remark by reminding myself that it wasn't her fault she had popping in and out issues, even if it happened during a private and potentially excellent moment. Instead, I responded to Logan's question. "One of the downsides to those abilities you thought were okay a few seconds ago."

"Are you telling me that Evelyn is here, now?" Logan gave the entire room a scrutinizing glance.

"Yes, but she has a tendency to vanish when startled, so if you could avoid using your interrogating tone…maybe continue using your charming boyfriend voice, I'd really appreciate it."

"You like my voice?" Logan straightened his shoulders and grinned.

He had a deep, rather sexy voice even when he was in detective mode, but I wasn't about to tell him and bolster his ego even more.

Evelyn crossed her arms. "So, what did I miss? Did you get a chance to ask him if he's going to help us? Did you tell him the necklace that was stolen was a fake and that the real one is hidden in the urn, not the safe?" She rambled a recap of what she'd told Jade, Shawna, and me when we'd returned to my apartment. "Oh, and is he going to let you have Daniel?"

"No, I didn't get a chance to ask him if he'd help us or tell him about the necklace, or the urn, or the secret staircase," I said.

"What secret staircase?" Evelyn's hands went to her hips. "And why didn't you tell me about it?"

"Sorry, I forgot you'd disappeared before we found it the night we were searching your house."

"Rylee." Logan had been listening intently and latched on to the part about me being in Evelyn's house and glared at me with his intense detective eyes, not his caring boyfriend gaze.

"Oops." I looked away from him long enough to make sure Evelyn hadn't left. "Remember our little talk about being charming, calming, and soothing?"

Logan glanced past his shoulder as if he'd actually be

able to see Evelyn. "She didn't…"

"Not yet…"

"Fine," he said in a softened tone. "I thought we agreed you weren't going to do any more breaking and entering."

"Technically, I had the owner's permission to go inside." I offered him an apologetic smile and held up my hand. "And, I didn't break anything while I was there, I swear."

"Logan's quite handsome when he does that serious thing with his eyes," Evelyn said.

I couldn't tell her I agreed with her, not without explaining to Logan what she'd said.

"All right, I guess we can let it go this time," Logan said. "Now, what was it you were saying about needing my help with a necklace and an urn?"

CHAPTER THIRTEEN

"I don't know how they do it," I grumbled as I adjusted the collar on my coat to keep my neck covered and the cold air off my skin.

"Do what?" Jade asked.

"Spend an entire night staking out a place." It had only been a few hours, and I was ready to go home and go to bed with my cat snuggled up on the comforter next to me.

When Logan said he'd be happy to help catch Evelyn's killer and didn't have a problem with Shawna, Jade, and I helping, I should have asked him to be more explicit. I had assumed my friends and I would be waiting inside the house with him and Roy, not sitting in the front of Gary's truck and parked beside his cottage with the engine turned off.

Logan had voiced his concerns on numerous occasions about how he disapproved of me doing any amateur investigating. I was convinced he'd made my friends and me stay outside because he knew we'd be sitting here freezing and probably hoped it would deter us from any future sleuthing.

It was my own fault for neglecting to tell him that my ghostly visitors would end up haunting me if I didn't help them resolve their unfinished business.

It was a good thing my parents and Grams had volunteered to work the final night of the haunted house. I could only imagine where Logan would have made them wait if they'd insisted on being here to help us.

Gary had offered to let us wait inside his home before heading off to visit a relative, but none of the windows faced the back yard of the main house or gave us a good view of the bushes concealing the secret staircase.

For our plan to be successful, we had to come up with a way to lure Harold to Evelyn's home. We also had to make sure that Kevin didn't know what we were doing or that we suspected his uncle of murder.

We were going on the assumption that whoever had taken the necklace already knew it was a fake and wouldn't pass on the opportunity to steal the real one. Roy and Logan decided the easiest way to handle the situation was to inform Kevin, Lydia, and Harold that the police tape was being removed, and they were releasing the crime scene the following day.

Since Roy had known Evelyn's family the longest, he was the one who'd made the calls. He wanted to keep the information as close to the truth as possible. He'd also told them that during their investigation they'd discovered a safe hidden behind some books in the library containing a necklace and some other valuable looking heirlooms, which were probably part of Kevin's inheritance.

In case one of them was aware of the necklace's real secret hiding place, he'd ended his conversation by telling them that Elliott had returned Daniel's urn to the mantle where Evelyn had always kept it. A conversation that so far hadn't produced any activity.

"It could be worse," Shawna said, distracting me from devising a way to get even with Logan later.

"How so?" Jade asked. She wasn't any happier about being stuck out in the cold than I was.

"We could be doing this without any food." Shawna

grabbed a chip out of the large bag we were sharing that she had sitting on her lap.

The melodic tune I'd assigned to Logan's cell number rang through the air, and I reached into my purse, which was tucked between my feet to retrieve my phone.

"Who's sending you a text?" Shawna bit into another chip and leaned closer.

"It's from Logan," I said. "He wants to know if we're doing okay and if we've seen anything yet."

"Awww." Shawna hovered near my shoulder so she could read the text. "I didn't know Logan had a mushy side."

I scrolled until I found an emoji of a snowman to send back to him, then returned the phone to my purse.

"How do you know Logan has a mushy side?" Jade asked. She was sitting on the other side of Shawna near the passenger door.

"He sent Rylee a cute smiley face emoji." Shawna grinned, no doubt logging the information into memory for use at a later, and beneficial to her, time.

Nate sent Shawna texts filled with emojis all the time, something Jade constantly teased her about.

"What if we're wrong about Harold being the one who hurt Evelyn?" Jade asked as she stuck her hand inside the bag to grab a chip before Shawna ate them all. "What if he doesn't show up and try to steal her necklace?"

"Honestly, I don't know who else it could be." Gary, Kevin, and Vivian all had plausible alibis. Even Lydia, who I would have suspected because of her spiteful attitude, had publicly announced her alibi to the police when she'd burst into Evelyn's foyer.

The thought of Evelyn being stuck in our realm because we couldn't find her killer was a possibility I didn't want to contemplate. She deserved to move on so she could be with Daniel.

Logan also told us he had to catch the person responsible in the act of actually trying to take the necklace, which was why he and Roy were hiding somewhere in Evelyn's home. Where it was warm.

Since my friends and I weren't allowed to be in the house, I'd picked our location because I thought Harold would walk over from the Beaumont. I hadn't expected to hear an engine rumble or have a car approach us using the back road that Evelyn had shown us.

"Get down," I said, then scooted lower in my seat seconds before the vehicle's high beams bounced through the cab.

"Do you think he saw us?" Jade asked. She was pressed against the door with her body hanging off the seat, her legs jammed underneath the dashboard.

The car used the small area next to the truck to turn around, so it was facing the direction it had come from. When it was about ten car lengths away from us, the driver parked and shut off the vehicle's lights.

"I hope not." Shawna's head was on my shoulder, her hair tickling my cheek.

"Why isn't he getting out of the car?" I asked after five minutes of being scrunched in the same position.

"That's a good question." Jade sounded as annoyed as I felt. "You'd think he'd want to get in and out of the house as quickly as possible, not take his time and risk Gary coming back early."

"Or maybe it's because he has help, and that's his getaway driver," Evelyn said after sticking her head through the windshield. The rest of her glowing form was sitting cross-legged on the hood of the truck.

I found the sight disturbing in a humorous way instead of a scared-and-should-be-shrieking way and had to clamp a hand over my mouth to keep from bursting into hysterical giggles.

"Rylee, what are you doing?" Shawna asked, shifting her head to see my face because I'd caught some of her hair with my hand. "Are you okay?"

"Yeah," I answered, then spoke to our ghostly visitor.

"Hey, Evelyn, what do you mean that's not him?" She was supposed to be inside watching the sliding panel on the second floor.

"Because I just saw him in the house, and he has Daniel's urn." Her furrowed brow and pursed lips were a perfect combination for the ghoul costume she was wearing.

Thinking it would be safe, we'd put Daniel's resting place on the nightstand in Evelyn's bedroom. "If he has the urn, then he must have known the real necklace is hidden inside." What I wanted to know was how and if the urn had been the intended target he been trying to steal the day he pushed Evelyn down the stairs. Maybe ending up with the fake necklace had been a mistake. And perhaps Grams and I had arrived before he could retrieve the urn.

"For those of us who are trying to keep up, who has the urn?" Jade snapped. Apparently, being contorted like a pretzel made her cranky.

"Harold," I exclaimed.

"Then who's driving that car?" Shawna hitched her thumb because it was easier than sticking out her arm, which would have ended up in Jade's face.

No longer concerned if I'd be seen, I grabbed my cell and sent Logan a text that said, "Harold in house. Has urn." I didn't have time to type in anything lengthy and assumed Logan would understand my cryptic meaning.

"Maybe we should find out." Gary's keys were already in the ignition, so after a quick turn and a pump on the gas pedal, the engine sputtered to life. "Hang on, Evelyn!" I shouted.

Logically, I knew she couldn't get hurt but was reacting to the rush of adrenaline pulsing through my body. I cranked the wheel and romped on the accelerator. I didn't think the old truck Gary used for hauling and other odd jobs could keep up in a road chase, so I maneuvered past the car, then parked sideways to keep the other vehicle from going anywhere.

116

Other than hearing a surprised yelp from Evelyn, she'd done nothing more than roll off the hood and float to the ground.

"Rylee," Shawna snarled when I hit the brakes. She slapped her hands on the dashboard to keep from sliding off the seat. Jade didn't say anything, but she clutched the armrest and shot daggers in my direction.

"What do you think you're doing?" Shawna asked after I opened the door and hopped out of the truck.

"Making a citizen's arrest."

***

I wasn't sure if it was my street racer tactics or the way I'd forced open the driver's side door of the car before yelling, "Don't move!" had scared Vivian the most. Now that she was sitting on the sofa in Evelyn's library sobbing so badly she could hardly talk, I felt a little guilty. If she'd turned out to be Lydia, as I'd originally suspected during my brief bout of what Shawna and Jade had proudly dubbed hot sleuthing pursuit, I wouldn't have cared in the slightest.

I couldn't tell if Logan was impressed or irritated about the method I'd used to apprehend Vivian. So far, I hadn't gotten a lecture, and until I did, I'd consider it a win. Roy hadn't said anything during my explanation either. The slight curve on the end of his lips told me he'd been amused but wouldn't openly admit it.

As for Harold, Logan caught him trying to abscond with the urn by using the secret staircase. He was currently sitting on a cushioned chair angled perpendicular to the sofa, nervously twisting his hands in his lap, his gaze darting around the room.

Logan had confiscated Daniel's urn and placed it back on the mantle above the fireplace where it belonged.

Evelyn ran her hand along the shiny metal, an appreciative smile on her face. "Please tell Logan I said thank you for rescuing Daniel. The necklace might be worth a lot of money, but my husband's ashes are priceless."

Roy wasn't aware of Evelyn's presence or that I could speak to her. I decided to wait until I was alone to pass on her thanks to Logan. I gave her an acknowledging nod, which she seemed to interpret correctly.

"I still can't believe Vivian is his accomplice." Hearing the devastation in Evelyn's voice made me wish I could give her a hug. It seemed as if Evelyn had been shaking her head nonstop since we'd escorted Vivian inside the house. If she'd still been alive, I was sure she'd end up with a kink in her neck.

It had to be difficult to discover that someone you trusted was complicit in taking your life. Of course, not everyone who died unnaturally ever learned the truth about their death.

Now that I was somewhat relaxed from my adventure, I still wasn't ready to take a seat, so I stood with Shawna and Jade next to one of the walls lined with shelves and filled with books.

Logan told my friends and me we didn't need to stay while he and Roy waited for an officer to arrive and escort Harold and Vivian to the station.

After everything we'd been through to help solve this case, there was no way I was leaving without hearing their explanation. An explanation I wasn't sure was going to happen since it didn't appear as if Logan or Roy were going to do any questioning until they got Vivian and Harold alone in an interrogation room.

Fortunately, I'd had the foresight to send my grandmother a text to let her know what had happened. Grams didn't care about police procedures and was a pro at the art of manipulation. It was apparent both techniques had been applied to poor Elliott when she rushed into the room ahead of him. They must have come from the haunted house because they both had on the same costumes they'd been wearing the night Shawna, Jade, and I had taken our partial tour.

"Are you girls okay?" The determined glint in Grams's dark eyes softened when she spoke to my friends and me.

"We're fine," I said, not bothering to ask her why she was here since I already knew.

Satisfied, she ignored Roy and Logan and focused her attention on Vivian and Harold. "Why did you do it?"

"Grams," Roy interceded by stepping in front of her. "Maybe we should go outside."

Elliott stood next to Jade, trying to stay out of the way and wait for Roy or Logan to tell him what to do. Logan had crossed his arms and seemed fine with letting his uncle handle things.

"I'm not going anywhere until these two tell me why they killed my friend." Grams tipped her head to the side to see past Roy and glare at Harold.

"We never meant for Evelyn to get hurt. We just wanted to be together." Vivian swiped at the tears gushing down her face. Her sniffles had transformed into heavy sobs, and I was afraid if Grams asked her another question, the girl would start wailing.

"Be together?" I hadn't planned to say anything, but my curiosity had other ideas.

"You've met my wife. You've seen how nasty she can be," Harold snarled.

"Why not just divorce her?" I asked.

"I couldn't, not if I wanted to keep the business I've spent most of my life working to build." Desperation laced Harold's tone. "I'd made the mistake of investing the money she'd inherited from her father, then let her talk me into making her a partner."

Harold gave Vivian a tender glance. "Then I met Vivian during Evelyn's party last year. I visited her whenever I was in town on business, and before I knew it, we'd fallen in love."

"I knew Harold was miserable being married to Lydia, but I had no idea how bad it was or that he was secretly seeing Vivian," Evelyn said.

"What does any of that have to do with shoving Evelyn down the stairs?" Grams spoke directly to Harold now that Roy had taken a step back and was no longer blocking her view.

Shawna leaned closer and whispered, "She's good."

If the situation hadn't been so depressing, I would have snorted. Had Shawna forgotten all the times Grams had done the same thing to us when we were younger?

"Her fall was an accident. I didn't shove her," Harold ground his teeth.

"Then why did you use the secret staircase to get in the house?" I asked.

"I just wanted the necklace," Harold said.

"What for?" Grams asked. "It wasn't worth anything?"

"Not the one she was wearing," Harold growled, seemingly losing patience. "I wanted the one Daniel gave her for their wedding anniversary. The valuable one she kept in the bottom of his urn."

I hadn't gotten a chance to tell Grams about Evelyn's fake necklace or where she kept the real one. When she gave me an inquiring glance over her shoulder, I returned it with an I'll-explain-later look.

"Everyone in my family had been at the anniversary party and seen Daniel give me the necklace, but none of them knew where I kept it." Evelyn went back to shaking her head at Harold again.

"How did you find out Evelyn kept the necklace hidden in the urn?" I asked.

"I told him," Vivian said. "I saw her putting it inside the compartment under the urn one day when I was cleaning downstairs." She started sobbing again. "I wasn't spying or anything, I swear. I didn't even know the necklace was worth a lot of money until Harold told me."

"And the secret panel…" I asked.

"That was me as well," Vivian answered again. "I found it by accident a few months ago when I got up on a chair to dust the picture frame."

"It's not Vivian's fault," Harold snapped. "After she told me what she saw, I knew I'd found a way to solve our problems without anyone getting hurt."

"Really?" Grams fisted her hands against her thighs. "I'll bet Evelyn would strongly disagree with you."

"Look, none of this would have happened if Evelyn had gone into town for her reading like she normally did," Harold said.

"No." Roy took a step forward to keep my grandmother from lunging at Harold. "This never would have happened if you hadn't tried to take something that didn't belong to you."

Roy's words of wisdom had created a room filled with silence. It took the longest time before Harold finally responded. "You're right. I'm sorry." The words came out raspy and pitiful, but believably sincere. He slumped his shoulders and went back to staring at the floor.

"Oh, Harold," Evelyn muttered.

I'd expected to see a mixture of anger and disappointment when I glanced at her face. Instead, what I saw was relief with a glint of sadness before she disappeared.

CHAPTER FOURTEEN

With the help of my friends, I'd survived and solved my third ghostly adventure. I'd even accepted the fact that I was going to have spirits popping into my world for the rest of my life. Eventually, the truth would come out, and everyone in town would know my secret.

I still hadn't decided the best way to handle it. Planning for the future was something I would deal with later after I'd had a long discussion with my family and friends. Right now, my main focus was saying goodbye to Evelyn, or at least to her ashes. I hadn't seen her since she'd disappeared the night we found out Harold and Vivian were responsible for her death.

Evelyn had included a final wish in her will; to have her ashes tossed over the side of the bluff along with Daniel's. I considered it a private occasion meant for family, but Kevin had insisted that Grams, Shawna, Jade, and I be there. He'd even asked Logan to attend since he'd played an important part in apprehending Harold and helping Evelyn find resolution so she could move on to the afterlife.

"Are you ready?" Kevin asked. He was standing next to me holding Daniel's urn.

"Yeah," I said, pulling the lid off the matching urn Kevin had purchased for Evelyn, less the box with a hidden compartment underneath.

He gave me a nod, and we simultaneously emptied the contents. As if by magic, a breeze carried the ashes away from the rocky ledge, then deposited them into the waves splashing against the rocks below.

Helping a spirit move on to their afterlife came with mixed emotions. The exhilaration from solving a crime faded when it came to saying goodbye. Logically, I knew it was inevitable, but it didn't make the situation any easier. Evelyn reminded me a lot of Grams. I was just getting used to her wearing kooky costumes and randomly shadowing me.

I knew it had to be even harder on my grandmother. The two women had been friends for decades. When Grams swiped at a tear, I reached over and squeezed her hand, gaining me an appreciative smile.

Evelyn appeared in the air over the bluff, this time wearing a regular skirt and blouse, but still a shimmering blue. Since Daniel had died from natural causes and moved on after his death, I was stunned to see his spirit arrive a few seconds later. As soon as he took Evelyn's hand and smiled, they both slowly faded.

Logan leaned closer, and in a low voice asked, "Are you okay?"

I didn't know if he was totally convinced that I could communicate with spirits, but it was nice to have his support nonetheless. "Yeah," I said, then faced the group. "Evelyn's with Daniel now."

"I know that's what everyone assumes, but how do you know?" Shawna asked.

My infuriating friend's question pulled me from my melancholy state and stopped any tears I might have shed. "Because I saw him ride up on a white horse and whisk her away through the pearly gates." I struggled to keep a grin off my face.

"Seriously?" Shawna's eyes got big, and she searched the sky in hopes of seeing the imaginary mount.

Jade tapped Shawna's arm with the back of her hand. "She's kidding." Then she glanced at me. "You are kidding, right?"

I giggled. "Yes, about the horse and the gates. Daniel did appear, but he took Evelyn's hand, and they disappeared together."

Shawna groaned. "We really need to find a way to see ghosts with you. It's too bad the spirit seeker only had enough juice for one person."

"What would you do if you could see ghosts?" Jade asked.

"Hmm." Shawna squinted and tapped her chin. "I'd probably open up a ghost detective agency. You know, someone who helps the newly departed. Or visits haunted houses and helps the spirits move on." She took a breath. "Oooh, and what if I could break curses? That might be a great business draw for the witching community." She flashed a mischievous grin in my direction. "Hey, maybe you should…"

"Oh, no, no, no," I stated emphatically by waving my hands. "Don't even think about it."

"Come on." Jade interceded, slipping her arm through Shawna's and dragging her in the direction of the vehicles parked in front of Evelyn's, now Kevin's, house. "Let's let Rylee say her goodbyes in peace. We can discuss her future sleuthing career later."

I wasn't sure how I felt about Jade passively supporting Shawna's suggestion. Having a debate with one of them at a time I could handle. Things got way more complicated when both of them disagreed with me. I could hear their mumbled voices, but not what they were saying, and assumed the conversation about my future hadn't ended when they left.

"You know she's going to check the Internet when she gets home to see if there is such a thing, right?" Grams chuckled.

"Yeah, I know."

Kevin lifted his elbow to Grams. "Shall we?"

"We shall." Before tucking her arm through his and following my friends, Grams took Evelyn's urn from me, then clutched it to her chest.

Logan gave my hand a squeeze. "I'll wait for you back at my truck."

"Okay," I said and continued staring at the waves.

"Rylee." Evelyn's ghost reappeared next to me. "Before I leave, I wanted to say thank you. If it hadn't been for you and your friends, I might not have found Daniel again."

"I'm glad we could help."

"Oh, and if you wouldn't mind, can you do one more thing for me," she asked.

The task could be anything, and I hesitated before saying, "I suppose."

"I worry about my boys. Promise me you'll check in on Kevin and Brutus now and then."

"That I can do." Though, judging by the way Kevin and Jade acted whenever they were together, I had a feeling I'd be seeing a lot more of him anyway.

I heard a faint thank you on the wind as her spirit vanished for the last time. Relief and the feeling of accomplishment accompanied me on the way back to the house, and I wondered if this was how Logan felt after solving a case.

I found him leaning against his truck with his arms crossed. As soon as his gaze locked with mine, he smiled and walked toward me. "Now that I'm officially dating a spirit sleuther, I think we need to have a discussion about what I should expect in the future." Logan took my hand. "Maybe over some coffee and one of those chocolate desserts dripping with caramel from Mattie's."

I grinned as I climbed into the passenger seat of his truck. "Have I ever mentioned how much I like the way you think?"

<<<<>>>>

ABOUT THE AUTHOR

Nola Robertson grew up in the Midwest and eventually migrated to a rural town in New Mexico where she lives with her husband and three cats, all with unique personalities and a lot of attitude.

Though she started her author career writing paranormal and sci-fi romance, it didn't take long before her love of solving mysteries had her writing cozies. When she's not busy plotting her next adventure, she spends her time reading and doing yard work.

CPSIA information can be obtained
at www.ICGtesting.com
Printed in the USA
LVHW081343231021
701307LV00015B/507

9 781953 213112